the
DEVIL'S
SUBMISSION
THE FALLEN SERIES

Happy Reading!

Nicola.

the DEVIL'S SUBMISSION

THE FALLEN SERIES

nicola davidson

Entangled Publishing, LLC
2614 South Timberline Road
Suite 109
Fort Collins, CO 80525
Visit our website at www.entangledpublishing.com.

Scorched is an imprint of Entangled Publishing, LLC.

Edited by Kate Brauning
Cover design by Erin Dameron-Hill
Cover art from RNC & Shutterstock

Manufactured in the United States of America

First Edition February 2017

entangled
scorched

To my CP, Sherilee Gray, for being amazing. To Jackie Ashenden, for the best pizza parties ever.

And to my faithful readers around the globe – your support and encouragement is very much appreciated.

Chapter One

"You must return to London, Eliza. It will be the *ton* wedding of the year!"

Lady Eliza Deveraux glanced again at the crisp gold-embossed invitation her mother, Countess Brimley, kept shoving under her nose. That Sin and his bride-to-be Grace had included her on the guest list warmed her heart no end. But under no circumstances would she be going. Not when attendance would put her in the vicinity of her estranged husband, Lord Grayson Deveraux, Sin's closest friend and second co-owner of the shockingly infamous pleasure club Fallen.

"No, Mother. I'll send them a gift and my deepest regrets; however, London and I do not get along."

"But the Prince Regent is a guest! And the Duke and Duchess of Waverly…oh, anyone who is anyone received an invitation. And if you go, Brimley and I can go with you."

"I said no. And that is the end of the discussion."

Lady Brimley glared at her. "You selfish, selfish, girl. Denying your father and me an opportunity like this because of your own gross failures. When I saw the betrothal announcement in the newspaper, I knew they would invite you. I waited and waited for you to share the news. But you chose to break my heart instead. What did I do to deserve the worst daughter in England?"

Gritting her teeth so hard they would soon grind to powder, Eliza fought to remain calm. To keep her tears unshed. To sip her tea rather than dump it on her mother's perfectly coiffed head. The dozens of scathing letters about her broken marriage had been sufficiently infuriating, but clearly her replies hadn't been detailed or apologetic enough to keep her mother safely far away at Brimley Park. This morning the damned crested carriage had pulled up in a clatter of gravel and dust; the gray-faced fatigue of the Brimley servants suggesting the usual leisurely two-day journey had been completed much faster. Not to mention her mother hadn't even waited until she'd stepped inside to discuss the wedding invitation, as if all were well between them. "I'm sorry you feel that way, but Grayson and I have been living apart for six months, and it is far better like this. Civil, even."

"Oh, you headstrong fool," spat Lady Brimley. "Do you have any idea of the further damage you did me when you ran away from your own husband?"

"I didn't run away—"

"Close enough for the gossips. As if it wasn't bad enough you set your heart on a scoundrel and married him because you thought you were in *love*. Sweet-talked your papa into countenancing a small, intimate wedding away from the *ton*. I might have borne that in time. Lord Grayson's enormous wealth, and his social connections do somewhat fade the stain of his filthy trade and scandalous reputation. But!"

Eliza stared longingly out the window. The balcony wasn't

so high; surely the shrubbery would break her fall. At least then she wouldn't have to listen to a lecture heard a thousand times already. "But he decided I should not reside under the same roof as him."

"Yes! Yes, he did! And now I am destroyed. Finished. Ended. An object of pity and scorn!"

"Oh dear." She sighed, wishing she could select the delectable-looking glazed jam tart from the tea tray. But provoking her mother's second favorite lecture — Eliza's Troublesome Weight — would not be a smart decision.

"You wretched girl! Have you no sorrow for my humiliation? The reputation of the Brimley Finishing Academy is ruined. We were renowned for our successes. As the sign stated, 'well-bred young ladies taught to be Delightful, Decorous, and Demure in preparation for excellent marriages.' But what *ton* mother will send her offspring to a school when the patroness's own daughter was such a terrible wife her husband couldn't stomach her so soon after the wedding?"

Eliza winced as a familiar pain clawed her heart.

Even now it was impossible to pinpoint what she'd done to make Grayson hate her so. From the moment she'd met the most handsome spectacle-wearing and ledger-loving lord in England, she'd been smitten. Twenty-eight years old, six feet tall, with a lean, muscled build, strong jaw, short-cropped ebony hair, and emerald green eyes to drown in. Oh, there had been the odd warning: that his nickname Devil was not only a play on his surname, but also an accurate description of an ice-cold bastard with the blackest of hearts. That he'd been disowned by his parents, the Marquess and Marchioness of Reyburn, for something so awful it was spoken of by no one.

But in the weeks of charmingly clumsy waltzes, long walks, rare flowers, and sizzling kisses, all that had seemed ridiculous, and she fell helplessly in love. For heaven's sake, Grayson had even tolerated her terrible tendency to issue instructions and discuss unladylike topics. Some of the shockingly risqué conversations they'd had…but those had paled in comparison to an unforgettable evening in the Brimley Park maze. She forgot herself completely, ordered him to touch her properly, and by heaven he'd obeyed. After Grayson had lowered her bodice and suckled her tender nipples, he'd lifted her gown and stroked the damp heat between her legs until she experienced her first shuddering climax. Unfortunately she came loudly enough for them to be discovered shortly afterward, but Grayson hadn't even waited for a *ton* trial. He'd immediately proposed, and they'd wed by special license three days later.

Cracks soon appeared. Her mother began visiting every second day to offer reminders and advice on how to be a worthy wife. Although Eliza tried her hardest to quell her stubborn, independent streak and be feted as a good and obedient Brimley Finishing Academy graduate, it seemed she could never reach the expected standard of decorum or submissiveness. The more she bowed to Grayson's will, the more he pulled away, spending increasing amounts of time in his office at Fallen with his guinea piles and ledgers, even taking a chamber there rather than returning to their townhouse. The nights he did come home, he reached for her less and less. And then came the awful day when she suggested a holiday and he counter-offered with a choice of property and a generous allowance if she left at once. She'd chosen the estate farthest away from London, a two-day carriage ride to just north of Gainsborough. And she'd fled.

The clattering of a teaspoon on fine bone china startled her out of her reverie, and she mumbled quickly, "Surely, Mother, the academy could not be doing as badly as all that."

"It is," Lady Brimley snapped. "Withdrawals are coming in by the day now, especially with summer upon us. All because you couldn't do your duty in *any* way. Twenty-four years old and still childless. The shame!"

"That wasn't my fault!" Eliza said hotly. "To conceive, your husband must actually share your bed. And after a while he…he didn't want to. He didn't want *me*."

"Because you are a twit. A brassy, outspoken hoyden who chose the wrong husband and then drove him away. I bet his mistress soothed him with quiet sweetness. Mrs. Lewis, wasn't that her name?"

Misery lodged in Eliza's stomach. It seemed everyone but her had known about Grayson's longtime paramour, Charlotte Lewis, who even had her own chamber at Fallen. How many nights when she'd lain alone had she tortured herself with images of him kissing the beautiful, slender brunette. Sucking her nipples. Kneeling between her spread thighs and licking her core. Penetrating her deeply with that long, thick erection of his, taking her hard, whispering words of love in her ear as they climaxed together.

"Perhaps," she choked out.

"Well then. This wedding is the perfect occasion to march back to London and prove you are more worthy than that trollop. If you would just style your unruly hair and commit to losing weight…Lord Grayson clearly prefers willowy to, er, rounded."

"I'm not returning to the capital, Mother."

"Yes. You. Are," Lady Brimley hissed. "Unless you want to see your own mother and father in the poorhouse?"

Eliza froze. "What on earth are you talking about?"

"We are two steps from ruin. Brimley made some bad investments and sank a great deal of money into some speculative stocks that Lord Grayson warned him to stay well away from. So I borrowed a little money from the school coffers. Just a temporary loan, you understand, not theft, and back then the academy wouldn't even notice it anyway. But thanks to you, the school is crumbling and the accounts are due to be checked next month!"

"Exactly how much money did you *borrow*?"

Lady Brimley's gaze darted away. "As I said, just a little."

"How. Much."

"Ten thousand pounds."

Eliza sank back on her chair. "Mother, you stole a blasted fortune!"

"Not to Lord Grayson," said her mother defensively. "The man could settle the debt with pocket change. And your husband owes us. He gained a wife far higher in birth than he deserved."

"What? Grayson is the son of a marquess!"

"The *disinherited* son. Listen to me, Eliza. If you were to go to London and attend the wedding, people might believe you had just been ill and needed complete rest in a very quiet place. Not a marriage failure at all. The academy would be saved on both fronts."

"And if he refuses and sends me packing within a minute?"

"Then I'll know you didn't try. For heaven's sake, girl. After everything your father and I have done for you, attending a society wedding and asking your husband for ten thousand pounds are tiny favors. You have always been the problem. For once, you can be the solution."

Eliza closed her eyes.

Oh, how she would love to tell her mother to go bathe in the Thames, especially when the woman demanded the impossible. To just saunter in Fallen's front door and announce "darling, I'm home, and by the by, might I have a bank draft?"

Grayson would happily toss her out. And yet he was the only person who could avert disaster. The thought of her sweetly absentminded papa locked in debtor's prison was too awful to contemplate.

Taking a deep breath, she opened her eyes and nodded.

"Very well. I'll go."

• • •

LONDON

"You cannot do this, Devil. You *cannot*."

Lord Grayson Deveraux tilted his head and stared dispassionately at the red-faced peer leaning over his office desk. The only thing vaguely intimidating about the man's stance was the threat of that too-tight, sweat-stained shirt splitting and revealing a sight from which his eyes would never recover. "On the contrary, Mandell. I can and I have."

"For a maid? A wretched no-name whore? If she had any sort of intelligence, she would know what an honor it was that I even looked at her, let alone touched her!"

"Perhaps other establishments encourage and celebrate such a mindset," Devil said coldly. "But at Fallen, everything, and I mean *everything*, is lady's choice. If a member disregards the rule of consent, his or her membership is terminated instantly. No refund."

Mandell thumped his fist on the oak desk. "Damned insolent pup! I am a marquess. I deserve a second chance, at least."

Devil folded his arms, lest he lose his temper and stab the man with his pen. Only the thought of stains on the Aubusson rug and the extra work for the parlor maids held him back. "Your rank is of no consequence, my lord. And second chances are not a custom I indulge in. The contract you signed clearly outlined all the club's non-negotiable rules; you break a rule, the privilege of membership is withdrawn. I assure you, Mandell, you and your documented underwhelming appendage from now on will be no more than an amusing tale here. So, you may either leave quietly or be thrown out. I'm sure our eminent Portman Square neighbors will enjoy the exhibition. Of course, I would then be forced to invoice you extra for the bother incurred."

The marquess's face went from purple to parchment. "My God. You would, wouldn't you? I never truly believed the rumors. I mean look at you: disheveled, ink-spotted, spectacles…like an absentminded clerk. But you are the coldest of bastards. Reyburn is well rid of you. As is your runaway wife."

Devil rose slowly to his feet. "Good day, Lord Mandell."

"G-good day, Lord Grayson," choked out the older man as he backed away and practically sprinted from the room.

Slumping against the edge of his desk, Devil took several deep breaths to calm his racing heart. Confrontations like those never got any easier, but damned if a fucking marquess of all people might get away with harassing one of the maids. Fallen was not only a pleasure club, but also a sanctuary for both staff and members, where no matter what happened outside the doors, inside was safety and freedom to explore.

Few people in the world knew it had always been a sanctuary for him as well.

He shuddered and ran a weary hand over his face, sighing at the sight of a blue smear on his fingertips. Hell and damnation. He really did need soap and water to remove the ink, and a change of clothing. When immersed in handling accounts, balancing the complex ledgers, settling bills, and counting out piles of coins for expenses and wages, such mundane tasks tended to fall by the wayside.

Eliza used to prompt you. Remember the time she dragged you into the bathing antechamber, stripped and soaped you all over? You pulled her into the copper tub fully clothed and "washed" her nipples and pussy with your fingers, then spent the rest of the night buried deep inside her perfect, lush body.

Devil clenched his fists, the urge to break something unbearable. He'd finally reached a point where he didn't think about his estranged wife every hour of every bloody day, and

Mandell had to go and remind him. From the moment he met Eliza during a solitary ride along Rotten Row, he'd been hooked. Became convinced she was strong, smart, feisty, and fearless, a woman whom he might in time share his deepest, darkest shame with. A woman who would free him with her loving care. As for their erotic courtship banter and kisses, the way she commanded like an empress...hell, he hadn't even cared when they'd been caught in a very compromising position in the garden. He'd been so eager to wed her he'd gone straight to the archbishop for a special license.

But not long after the wedding, everything changed. He found himself married to a timid, bland, and cool society princess, one who turned even more proper and particular as the weeks went on. All the confusion, self-doubt, and anger swirling in his mind had been bad enough. But when the tension increased to the point he couldn't even get hard anymore, the knowledge that he was less than a man became unendurable. His parents were right. He was weak, a disgusting aberration, a stain on the Deveraux name.

So he'd sent Eliza far away, thinking it would solve everything, that he'd finally be able to sleep and fuck and laugh again. But it hadn't worked. He lived like a damned vampire monk, buried in bookwork and occasionally visiting the activity rooms to watch a performance with his club co-owners and closest friends, Sin and Vice. Only to return to his chambers, scrub himself raw, take a few bottles of brandy to bed, and attempt to drink himself to blessed oblivion. Sometimes it worked. Sometimes he stared at the ceiling for hours and wondered if it might be easier to end it with a knife or rope rather than exist a day longer in this empty, angry, false half life.

"You are a truly pathetic oddity," Devil muttered, so ready for sleep even the solid oak under his backside tempted him to sprawl across it.

Several frantic, heavy knocks on the door ended that fantasy.

"Devil!" yelled a muffled female voice. "Devil, come quick!"

Frowning at the urgency, and something suspiciously like excitement, in the maid's voice, he inched toward the door. Sleeping in his office was a bad idea anyway. Hell, last time he'd done it, six maids turned feral and took him hostage.

"Just a minute," he called back, ambling to the door, unlocking it, and peering around. "What is the matter?"

The maid bobbed a curtsy and beamed. "Oh, it's the best news. Lady Eliza is here for Sin and Lady Carrington's wedding!"

Devil froze, staring uncomprehendingly. "What?"

"Your wife, sir," she repeated at a slower pace, as if he were hard of hearing rather than staggering from a sucker punch. "Lady Eliza has finally come home, trunks and all, and asked to see you at once. She's just refreshing herself in your chamber."

"All right," he said quickly. "I'll be there soon."

Christ.

Closing the door, he leaned against it, shock and dismay and hope swirling in his head so fast it made him dizzy. And aroused. Fuck, how could that even be? Countless nights of watching naked women and crops and toys and shows, and he'd gotten semi-hard at most. Eliza in the same building and his cock was about to split his trousers. Damned idiot appendage. Courtship Eliza, the one who had taken charge and pleasured him senseless, was a myth. A trick. The wife who awaited him down the hallway was a different woman entirely.

With a low curse, Devil swiftly undid his trousers and adjusted himself. Hopefully his cock would calm down before he got to his chamber, but he couldn't wait a minute longer.

The return of Eliza Deveraux, he had to see to believe.

• • •

Fallen hadn't changed a bit.

Walking through the front door and into the foyer had been like slipping into a quilted dressing gown and savoring a mouthful of particularly fine wine. So elegant, so utterly decadent, and yet so comfortably familiar, too, with the marble floor, shimmering glass chandelier, and collection of exquisite paintings lining the walls, even one that she had personally chosen.

But Grayson's lavish second-floor suite, once upon a time a newlywed haven of laughter and love and indescribable pleasure, would surely crush her with memories.

Early in their marriage she'd stayed here, despite her mother's vocal protests. It had almost been amusing at the time, as it wasn't the club Lady Brimley protested about—the wealth it created, along with its rumored list of *haut ton* patrons, quelled that—but Eliza's "bluestocking activities" like filing paperwork, settling expense lists, and creating drafts because of Grayson's truly appalling handwriting.

It was both embarrassing and troubling to recall how much she had loved her bizarre, busy, and unconventional life. Especially when it was the reason the marriage failed. Every time her mother had visited, she had warned Eliza that her interference in men's matters, her crowding, and tendency to instruct Grayson spelled doom. She should instead be demure and submissive. With every warning she had tried harder, taken part less, even dutifully retired to Grayson's scarcely used townhouse. But she had missed him terribly. And even though the townhouse was perfectly lovely, it reminded her too much of Brimley Park and the academy. Lovely shells with no heart. No warmth. No joy or air of welcoming sanctuary. It had never felt like *home.*

Not like this enormous, sprawling, three-storied red-brick structure in the heart of Portman Square. As soon as the Brimley carriage pulled up, footmen had dashed outside to help her with her belongings. Diaz, the frightening and formidable butler, actually smiled when he bowed over her hand. And dozens of maids, or the "harem" as Grayson always smilingly called them, squealed and cheered, clearly thinking this was a pre-planned, romantic, and heartfelt reunion. If only…

"Well, well. Eliza Jean Brimley Deveraux, as I live and breathe."

The cool words in that rough silk voice hung in the air behind her, and she stilled, almost afraid to turn around. But she did.

Oh God.

The impact of her husband was as powerful as ever. Still that jolt where her body begged for an immediate disrobing, combined with the heart clench that made her want to cradle him and smooth the tension from his brow. Grayson remained unbelievably handsome, although his cheekbones looked more prominent, as though he'd lost weight. Miracle of miracles, he'd actually shaved, but as always, he needed a soapy cloth and a freshly pressed shirt. The adorable ink spot on his nose where he absently pushed his spectacles higher was as prominent as ever. Unfortunately the remoteness, the suppressed anger, and the haunted pain she'd so desperately wanted to reach and heal endured also.

"Hello, Grayson," she said softly, yearning to hold him while achingly aware of how unwelcome her touch would be.

He ambled forward, one jerk of his head sending the trunk-depositing footmen scurrying on their way. "I'm a little surprised. Your last letter didn't mention any plans to come to London, nor did you send an acceptance of the wedding invitation. If I'd known, I would have made the townhouse ready."

So cold. So polite. Abruptly the character flaw her mother loathed reared its head, urging her to crack the mask, to make him feel something. "No need," she replied, smiling with determination. "Your chamber is most adequate. And if I have timed it with any luck, the left side of the bed should be currently vacant…"

Her voice trailed off, not in embarrassment, but at what her lowered gaze spotted. Grayson's trousers, incorrectly fastened, and a large bulge tenting the close-fitting fabric. Oh God. She'd interrupted him with a lover. Perhaps a temporary companion, or that woman, Charlotte, on her knees, stroking and sucking his thick length. Or maybe he'd been readying her, expertly licking and fingering between her legs while she moaned and arched in pleasure.

"Something the matter, Eliza?" he said, one eyebrow raised, his emerald green gaze suddenly gleaming.

"Not at all," she gritted out, hating the woman, whoever and wherever she was. "I didn't mean to disturb."

Grayson moved past her, then unexpectedly halted so he stood behind her. "Not at all, my dear," he said silkily, and it took every ounce of her will to stay upright and not melt at the brush of his hard lips against her ear. "We are well-versed in accommodating unexpected guests."

Eliza clenched her fists at the barb. "Oh, of course you are."

"Tart words from my timid wife," he replied. "If only you'd wanted to…damnation, Eliza, why are you here?"

"Sin's wedding," she said slowly, her heart pounding at the slight crack in his armor. Dare she push him further? "He invited me, based on our past friendship. Nothing to do with you."

"Rubbish. You would have sent a charming gift with your

deepest apologies. Something else prompted you."

Eliza licked bone-dry lips. Her blasted husband knew her entirely too well, but he forgot she knew him like the other half of her, too. And right now he balanced on an edge she could practically see. "I'm sure I don't know what you mean."

"Liar. Do you want me to petition parliament for a divorce? Or perhaps you are lacking a lover and wish to make use of Fallen. Well, my lady, I would point you in the direction of an activity room, but fucking a passionless and oh-so-proper society spouse is not a popular option. They want to leave those at home—"

The slap echoed through the chamber like a pistol shot. Eliza stared at her hand in shock, but the pink hue of her stinging palm confirmed she had indeed just hit her husband across the cheek. Her gaze flew to his, bracing for anger and disgust at the unforgivable act. Instead, she caught a flash of something dark and raw. Hopeful. Almost pleading? "Grayson…"

"Yes, Eliza?" he said in a voice she'd never heard: low and warm and rasping. He wasn't even making eye contact now but staring somewhere over her left shoulder, and his whole body was tense like a bow pulled taut, his erection undiminished.

A pulse thudded between her legs in the shrieking silence, and her nipples were so hard the muslin of her tea gown felt like sackcloth. All she wanted to do was kiss the mark she'd made. Haul Grayson over to the oversized four-poster bed, tear his clothes off, and take that thick erection deep inside her wet heat. Not passively underneath as usual, but riding him like a mount, gripping him, milking him, forcing him to release every drop of seed he had to give.

Owning him.

Horrified, Eliza jerked away, practically throwing herself across the room to slump onto the long embroidered chaise resting against the west wall. What kind of monster had she become? Hitting her own husband and being aroused by it?

"I'm sorry. I'm so sorry," she said hoarsely, tears welling in her eyes. "That was inexcusable. I don't even know what came over me. But it won't happen again, I promise."

Eventually Grayson turned and shrugged, yet an emotion lingered in his eyes that looked incredibly like hollow disappointment. How could that be?

"Forgotten already, my lady. Though should you tire of society life, you could probably make a few guineas in the ring. Pay a few spectators to rile that Irish temper of yours, and boom! Knock out, round one."

"That is not funny. I slapped you!"

"Indeed. I was here for the experience, and I deserved it. For all I know, you could have a dozen lovers and an entire room for feathers, beads, and toys."

Shaking her head quickly before the inexplicably alluring thought of sexual accessories could lodge in her mind, Eliza stood. "Again, I apologize, Grayson. If you'll just direct me to a guest room, I'll have my trunks moved in there and make myself scarce for the rest of the afternoon."

Grayson blinked, then scowled. "There are no spare chambers. All have been taken by Sin and Grace's out of town wedding guests until at least Saturday."

"Oh."

"I suppose we could share a bed tonight. I trust you'll keep your pugilistic impulses in check, even if I do mutter something in my sleep. Not at all sporting to hit an unconscious man, no matter how provoking he is."

She laughed. "I shall be a statue, I promise. You won't even know I'm here."

Instead of smiling in return, Grayson grimaced. "Oh, I'll know. Dinner is at eight. Do you wish to join everyone or have a tray in here?"

"A tray, if that is all right. Two days in a carriage and I'm quite exhausted."

"It's fine. I'll have one of the harem attend you. Until later, then."

The moment she was alone, Eliza buried her face in her hands. A half hour in Grayson's company, an argument, and she'd hit him. If she'd been smarter, she might have asked for the bank draft to save her parents while the handprint across his cheek still glowed. Then maybe broken a few priceless vases and insulted Sin, Grace, and Vice to really impress.

No way would this all end in disaster.

No way at all.

Chapter Two

As promised, Eliza slept soundly on the left side of the bed.

Well, not precisely on the left side anymore. During the night she'd inched closer and closer, and Devil was currently hard to the point of agony. Her citrusy scent surrounded him, locks of her wild, sunset-red hair spilled over his pillow, and as for her body—even a modest nightgown couldn't disguise her mouthwatering hourglass lushness.

"Grayson," she said. He froze, then sighed in relief at the realization she'd merely mumbled his name in her sleep. Until she rolled onto her side and tucked her head against the curve of his neck, allowing her breasts, those ample, dusky brown-tipped curves of perfection, to press against his naked chest. One tug of a satin bow and he could lick her left nipple. Suck it. Scrape it with his teeth. If he slid his hand down and lifted the hem of her nightgown just a few more inches, he could cup her mound. Part the crisp red curls, stroke her petal-soft labia, tease her clit until his fingers were soaked in her wetness and she arched and screamed his name…

Devil shuddered, muffling a groan.

All in all, he was in sexual hell. Had been for hours. The erection he'd sported upon learning Eliza had returned was nothing compared to now, when he relived the moment she'd disciplined him for his purposefully goading comment. The incredulous joy at the sharp crack and delicious, heated prickle exploding along his cheekbone. If Eliza had touched him anywhere, he would have come in his trousers. Obeyed any instruction she uttered. But while he'd been aroused beyond belief, his wife had been appalled and tearful.

Yet again, the crushingly familiar shame and guilt enveloped him. How typical, that the one woman who had gotten under his skin, who tormented him with glimpses of the power and authority he craved from her, wanted no part of it. But Eliza was in London for some damned reason other than Sin and Grace's wedding. It would just be a matter of extracting the truth from her before he became a prime candidate for Bedlam.

Closing his eyes, he breathed deeply. Even just a half hour's rest would be better than nothing.

"Grayson. Grayson! Wake up!"

He didn't open his eyes. That was not the tone used when one's wife was about to suggest hours of torrid and athletically amorous activity, and he couldn't think of another good reason to be awake. "Frightfully bad idea, my dear. It's the middle of the night."

Eliza's snort probably could have been heard down the hallway. "It's not the middle of the night; it is a quarter past ten in the morning. We are going to be late for the wedding if you don't get up right now."

Incredulous, he opened one eyelid the merest slit. But it was true. The heavy curtains were drawn, and golden sunlight streamed through the diamond-paned windows. Christ. He'd actually slept. "I'll be ready in twenty minutes. Well, as long as I don't strangle myself attempting to tie a cravat."

His wife tilted her head and shot him a curious look. "You still don't have a valet?"

Under the blankets, his fists clenched, and cold sweat gathered at the nape of his neck.

Don't react. Don't. She doesn't know about Reyburn's valet and his damned fists. Don't let her guess.

"No," he replied eventually, with a semblance of a laugh. Hell, even in his mind he couldn't bear to call the Marquess of Reyburn "Father," yet another entry on his pathetic list. "Never could be bothered. Still can't, no matter what society says."

Eliza grinned. "Anything other than charmingly crumpled wouldn't really be you. At least you've taught yourself how to shave. Your jaw looked positively civilized yesterday."

A genuine chuckle escaped this time. "Actually, I haven't. When I get too furry, Charlie marches me to a chair and attacks me with a razor blade. She's a dab hand, so I always try to stay on her good side."

"She? Oh. *Oh*. You mean Charlotte Lewis."

"Yes," he said crisply, irritated at the sudden coolness in his wife's voice and the frown creasing her brow. Not everyone had the good fortune to be born legitimate. "Her half brother was a soldier turned valet. Taught her well before he passed. I'll ring—"

"No need. I called for hot water, and it was delivered a few minutes ago. I'll help you with your cravat, then you can help me with my stays."

Devil raised an eyebrow at the unexpected offer, but he got out of bed and padded in his unfastened trousers over to the ceramic washbasin behind an embroidered screen. Stripping off the trousers, he swiftly washed himself with his preferred sandalwood soap, then pulled on the fresh shirt and trousers one of the maids had left hanging on a hook nearby. "All right, I'm decent."

Eliza stepped around the screen, a length of silky white fabric in her hands. "Well then, sit down so I can tie this properly. You're as bad as Papa when it comes to hating cravats."

Obediently, he perched on a comfortable leather-covered stool, and she began expertly winding the cloth around his neck. The position put her luscious breasts right in his face, and he almost groaned as they moved and jiggled in front of him. Hadn't he endured enough torture for one damned day?

"Hell," he muttered as his cock twitched.

"What? Is the cravat too tight?"

"No, it's fine. I'll wait out there while you wash."

Before he could escape, Eliza's slim fingers encircled his wrist. "Grayson. What is wrong?"

Devil started to reply with something false, something polite. But he was so goddamned weary of false and polite. "That nightgown is too small."

Her face fell. "I-I know. Mother says I'm too big, that if I just lost some weight…"

"Why the hell would you want to do that? Damnation, Eliza, it's not your weight, it's your fucking perfect breasts straining against the fabric. I was hard all night looking at that little bow, thinking how easy it would be to undo so I could take one of your nipples into my mouth and suck it until it was so swollen, so sensitive, you screamed."

Eliza's eyes widened, her cheeks pink. "Why…why didn't you?"

Because I want you to tell me to. To order me to pleasure you, like that time in your parents' garden maze. One of the few nights I felt free…

"You were asleep," he said eventually, looking away and feeling like a damned idiot. Sin and Vice, not to mention most other men in his acquaintance, would laugh themselves catatonic if they knew about this need in him. God knew

Reyburn had tried to beat the softness and weakness out after it had fully manifested in his last year at Eton, even requesting the masters never spare the cane. His younger son finding pleasure in pain was definitely a result the marquess neither expected nor wanted.

Warm lips brushed his cheek, and Devil jolted in surprise. Eliza's face was almost crimson now, but her gaze was defiant. Would she dare?

A moment later she sank down onto his lap, cupped his cheek in her free hand, and kissed him squarely on the mouth. It was a swift kiss, a chaste one, yet heat scorched a path from his lips to his cock.

"Grayson," she whispered, her soft lips brushing his ear. "Kiss me back."

With a guttural groan he pulled her close and captured her mouth with his. She whimpered, but she wasn't pulling away or flinching at his need. She was holding on and rubbing her breasts against his chest.

"Eliza," he said hoarsely, when he couldn't quite catch his breath.

"Do it." She tugged on the bow of her nightgown so hard it tore and revealed the curves of her plump breasts. "Do what you said you wanted to last night."

Transfixed, he lowered his head toward the bounty in front of him. "Your wish is my command."

• • •

She'd been bold. Bolder than she'd been in months, and heavens, what a reward.

Around and around, up and down, Grayson's lips were trailing across her breasts, his tongue a hot lash against her aching nipples. It felt so good all she could do was moan his name, and yet it wasn't nearly enough. "Suck me," she breathed.

He raised his head. "Beg pardon?"

"Suck me," she said, a bit louder, squirming in Grayson's lap when his hand rubbed slow circles against her lower back.

"Still can't hear you. *Lizzie*," he replied, his eyes so bright with uncharacteristic mischief, Eliza swallowed hard against an overwhelming rush of topsy-turvy emotion.

Grayson had first called her Lizzie the night in the Brimley Park maze. And continued to while their marriage worked. He was the only person in the world who had ever called her by a nickname, though she'd scolded him a thousand times for it: The Delightful, Decorous, and Demure ladies of the Brimley Finishing Academy simply did not stand for shenanigans with their names, or any other such social informalities. "Grayson…"

"Hmmm?" he said, circling her areola with the tip of his tongue.

Almost panting with need, all thoughts of proper behavior fleeing her mind, she cupped the back of his head and pushed it closer to her breast.

"Suck my nipples," she said fiercely. "Suck them hard… oh God, yes, just like that."

Every draw of Grayson's lips, every nip of his teeth sent an incredible jolt of heat straight to her core. Eliza writhed on his lap, almost insensible with pleasure. Between her legs she could feel the thick length of his erection nudging her, and she moaned as she ground herself against it.

"What else?" he gasped, the scorching hot lust in his eyes almost making her orgasm on the spot. "Tell me what else, Lizzie."

"Make me come."

He made a growling sound, his erection jerking hard against her. "You want me to rub your clit? Fill your pussy with my cock?"

"Both. Oh please, I want—"

They both froze as sharp knocks pounded on the chamber door, the wood creaking slightly as it swung open and a heavy footfall marched into the room. Thanks to the bathing screen, they were hidden from view.

"Devil. What the fuck are you doing?" yelled a man in a very familiar Scottish brogue. "The carriage is leaving in five…Devil? Are you in here?"

"Yes," called Grayson in a rather hoarse voice. "We'll see you in a minute, Vice."

"We? Oh. Good morning…Lady Eliza?"

"Yes, it's me," she snapped as she eased off Grayson's lap, supremely irritated at Vice's hesitancy over her name. Were there that many possibilities? Did her husband have a different woman in here every night of the blasted week?

"Ah. Well, we need to leave, my lady. It's a way to travel to the Archbishop's palace, and while Sin and Grace may forgive us our trespasses, the harem would deliver the evil in apocalyptic form if we were to mar the day in any way. You know they would. Not to mention Prinny and the rest."

"Very well," Eliza said crisply. "Give us just a moment."

As soon as the door shut behind Vice, she hurried over to the smaller of her trunks and took out a fresh chemise. She could hear her husband moving about the room behind her, combing his hair and slipping on a waistcoat and jacket, but she couldn't even look at him.

How many women had slept in this room? Had straddled Grayson on that same leather stool while he pleasured them beyond belief? Did Charlotte not only assist him with shaving, but also help him with the accounts, sponge the ink blotches, welcome him into her bed every other night?

Angry, jealous tears burned Eliza's eyes, but she refused to let them fall. That was a private pain.

"Shall I lace your stays?"

Eliza nodded, trying not to flinch at how close Grayson was as he threaded the silken cords and pulled them tight. Trying not to scream at the horrible jumble of thoughts twisting and turning through her mind as she tugged on a hunter-green striped muslin gown for the wedding.

Stepping into heeled slippers, she finally turned. "I'm ready. Do you need your spectacles?"

Grayson's lips quirked. "Only for bookwork. I'm not quite in my dotage yet. For instance, it is very clear right now that you look beautiful in that gown. Not quite as beautiful as in the nightgown with the torn bodice, but a very close second."

The tears burned again. Damn him. "Well then. Let's go before Vice leaves without us."

The carriage ride to the south bank of the Thames was surprisingly fast and uneventful, and Morton's Tower soon loomed above them. As Grayson escorted her into Langton's chapel within Lambeth Palace, the residence of the Archbishop of Canterbury, Eliza couldn't help a sneaking glance at her husband. The last time they had been here, crossing the black-and-white checkered marble floor, positively dwarfed by the stunning stained glass windows, it had been for their special-license wedding.

Grayson met her gaze and smiled. "Archbishop Manners-Sutton is going to be sick of the sight of us. Fortunately we keep making substantial donations to his favorite charities."

"Or he is a man with a soft spot for love, and who cares about his flock, even the worst rogues," she replied primly.

"That, too."

She, Grayson, and Vice barely had time to take their seats before the ceremony began. Sin, the handsome rake whom she only sometimes remembered to call Sebastian or Lord St. John, stood at the altar holding his beautiful betrothed Lady Grace Carrington's hands in his. They were both dressed so elegantly, Sin in black trousers and jacket with a sapphire blue waistcoat, and Grace in a heavenly gown of topaz silk, and the expressions on their faces were so joyful, so tender, it hurt to watch them pledge themselves to each other. Although by all accounts, Sin and Grace had endured a rocky path to this day and very much deserved their happy ending.

Grief gripped her. She had looked like Grace on her wedding day, so happy and hopeful and madly in love. The marriage foundering so quickly had been soul-destroying. Now kissing her husband, touching him, and seeing hints of the softer side he rarely showed anyone was just salt in the wound. If it weren't for her blasted mother, Eliza would never have put herself through this. When Grayson found out the real reason behind her being in London, he would shun her completely.

As the kindly archbishop continued the service, her gaze slipped around the chapel and widened at the sheer number of attendees from the very highest echelons of power. The Prince Regent sat with Mrs. Fitzherbert in the front row, next to the Duke and Duchess of Waverly, Grace's uncle and aunt. Prime Minister Liverpool sat a row back, along with several older peers who had probably been close friends of Sin's late parents, Lord and Lady St. John. Five rows behind them sat her own mother and father, Lady Brimley waggling her fingers and smiling broadly, no doubt in transports at the company she was keeping.

"With this ring I thee wed," said Sin in a loud, clear voice to complete the ceremony, "with my body I thee worship, and with all my worldly goods I thee endow. In the Name of the Father, and of the Son, and of the Holy Ghost. Amen."

Eliza applauded with the rest of the guests when a beaming Sin and Grace left the chapel as a married couple, but as the stragglers mingled and chatted, a hand clamped on her elbow and led her to the corner.

"Well, Eliza? Have you asked him?" hissed Lady Brimley

out of the side of her mouth while smiling and nodding at passersby.

"No. Not yet."

"What? Why not?"

She gritted her teeth. "We have been apart six months, Mother. I couldn't just demand ten thousand pounds on my first day back. Not when things are…uneasy."

"I can see that for myself," said her mother, nudging her so she turned left. "You promised me you would try, but there your husband is, all smiling and cozy with his mistress. How convenient, her being acquainted with Lord St. John and his new wife, so she could even attend the wedding."

Feeling like she'd been pummeled, Eliza glanced over to the other side of the chapel. Indeed, there the two of them were: her husband and Charlotte Lewis, bathed in a rainbow of light from a stained-glass window, their heads together as they spoke. "Grayson can talk to whomever he pleases."

"Of course. But they aren't talking, they are confiding. If you behaved like a proper wife, he would treat you like that. Then you could get the money. Go to him. Send that trollop on her way. Don't forget, though, a lady never raises her voice."

Eliza hesitated, weighed down by doubt. She hadn't behaved like a proper wife this morning, boldly ordering Grayson to do as she wished. And he'd lost his iron control. He'd smiled, really smiled, like he'd been happy, and kissed and touched her with such passion. But if he'd liked that so much, why was he now flaunting his close and intimate relationship with Charlotte? Again, it seemed her mother was correct. This morning had been a passing whim. Sweet, obedient Charlotte was the constant in Grayson's life, the woman he kept returning to. Unless she learned how to be like his lover, she didn't stand a chance.

Squaring her shoulders, Eliza walked toward them.

It was time to meet the enemy.

. . .

"Dev, if you want any chance at happiness, you have to tell her."

Devil glanced down at Charlotte, one eyebrow lifted in a very mocking slant. "You know as well as I do the monumental difficulties of that conversation. Besides, she doesn't want any part of it. She delivered the most exquisite slap, then nearly burst into tears."

The beautiful brunette, whom he owed his life to, heaved an audible sigh. "I'm quite devastated, you know. My record of nudging dominant women and submissive men together was, until you and Eliza, perfect. I spied on her several times when she rode in Rotten Row, and I was so sure I saw traits of myself...damnation. I should never have encouraged you to accidentally-on-purpose bump into her. I'm so sorry."

He shrugged. "Don't be. I thought I saw the traits in our courtship. Christ, Charlie, it was..."

"Amazing? Blissful?" Charlotte smiled sadly.

"All of the above. But enough about me. How goes the world with your latest paramour?"

"That is over," she said briskly, but he could see the hurt in her eyes. "The earl spun a good tale, but he was very lazy and entirely focused on pleasing himself rather than me. The first time I used my crop on him he punched me square in the stomach and said he'd kill me if I ever told anyone. I didn't tell Sin; I was too mortified."

Devil took her hand and squeezed it, ten years of friendship in the gesture. The illegitimate and unacknowledged daughter of a viscount, Charlotte had always lived on the fringes of society, too high class for the servants, and too low class for the nobility. She'd been an actress, then a courtesan, made some money, and purchased her own small townhouse from which she hosted parties of a very discreet and certain nature—where men could explore the various elements of their sexuality. He'd heard of her through a classmate at Cambridge and attended several of her parties. After Reyburn had thrown him out, he'd half crawled, half walked, bloodied and broken, to her doorstep. Charlie had taken him in, no questions asked, and he'd stayed with her until he reached his majority and inherited money from a maternal aunt.

When he'd started Fallen with Sin and Vice, she'd been the first person he'd offered a luxurious life and well-paid employment to, for as long as she wanted it.

"Bastard," he said fiercely. "But you know I love you unconditionally and for time without end, correct?"

Charlotte smiled and squeezed his hand back. "And I love you. Even if you keep me awake at night."

"Well, I never," said an icy voice behind him. "So much love in this chapel."

Dismayed, he turned on his boot heel. "Eliza. I'm not sure if you've met my very good friend—"

"I know who she is," his wife spat, her eyes a silver storm. "Mrs. Lewis."

"That's right," said Charlotte pleasantly. "I'm Charlotte. Or Charlie if you prefer. I always thought Mrs. Lewis sounded quite ridiculous considering I've never been married. Living with Dev was the closest I ever got."

"Perhaps it is time you did find a husband. Other than mine."

"Eliza," he said with a frown. "That is uncalled for."

"Hush, Dev," said Charlotte, surprising him. "In response, my lady, I can only plead the difficulties in finding a husband when you have certain…quirks."

"Such as you prefer men already married?" snapped Eliza.

Charlotte laughed. "Well, married men are often much less trouble. But I was actually referring to—"

"I don't care! You stay away. Actually, it would be far better if you packed your trunks and were gone from Fallen tonight."

Both women looked at him, Eliza all fire and brimstone, and Charlotte surprised irritation. Grayson silently cursed his wife's outburst, even as the possessiveness behind it warmed him to the core. This was so damned complicated.

"No," he said quietly but firmly. "Charlie has a home at Fallen for as long as she wants it."

"Fine. Fine," said Eliza, every part of her body screaming betrayal, hurt, and fury. "I'll leave you two alone, then."

As she hurried away, almost running from the chapel, Devil swore.

"Go after her, Dev," said Charlotte with a sigh.

"I'm not throwing you out. I won't. Ever. It's my fucking house. Eliza doesn't decide who lives there."

Charlotte glared at him. "Don't be a bloody fool. If it comes down to a choice, you choose Eliza, the woman you love, who also seems to have a great deal of feeling for you. Go."

"I'm not throwing you out," he repeated. "And I'll see you later at the club. It's past time I made an appearance."

Her eyes widened. "No, Dev…"

But he'd already turned away, crossing the black-and-white checkered floor and sprinting out of the chapel at such pace he almost got vertigo. Yet as he burst through the chapel doors, the only thing that greeted him was warm sunlight on his face, and the sight of his carriage pulling away with Eliza in the back.

Fuck.

Hailing a hackney, Devil returned directly to Fallen and locked himself in his office. Usually poring through the accounts, counting guineas, being enveloped in the scent of leather, parchment, and ink calmed him like nothing else.

But not today. Even when he forced himself to stay in the room rather than confront his wife, when the bright sunlight faded to dusk then darkened to night and a maid brought a tray with freshly baked bread, roasted chicken, creamed peas, and buttered potatoes, he ignored the clawing feeling of wrongness. Instead, he opened a third bottle of brandy while still staring at the same page of the same ledger he'd been staring at since he got home.

It's your fault. If you weren't so weak, so abnormal, your marriage would have worked. You would never have imposed on Charlie. Your parents and brother wouldn't consider you dead to them. You would have fought off the valet who helped beat you to a pulp...

Shuddering, Devil lifted the bottle and took several long swallows, welcoming the burn in his mouth and throat, the warmth that settled in his stomach. He could be alpha, the one in charge, he just hadn't been trying hard enough.

With the careful steps of a man who'd had too much brandy and not enough food, he left his office and walked downstairs, then across the foyer toward Fallen's main entrance. Diaz, their butler, looked at him with surprise and concern but wordlessly opened the heavy oak door for him, and he made his way through the main ballroom. The chandelier-lit space teemed with elegantly dressed people, all wearing numbered masks, laughing and enjoying themselves as they indulged in excellent food and wine, listened to the orchestra, and planned their sexual activities for the evening. Some would watch shows, some would indulge in the various pleasure rooms, others would swap spouses or be introduced to a new temporary lover.

He inclined his head and exchanged greetings with several members but didn't stop until he reached a chamber at the end of a narrow hallway. In this room a small group of alpha male exhibitionists met each week to play with, and show off, their exhibitionist wives. He could learn how to act, how to be effortlessly strong and forceful from these men. This was how it was supposed to be, after all.

"Well," Devil said harshly to the room of masked but naked men and women. "What do we have here?"

"Just some lovers about to indulge in friendly play," said Charlie, who stood to his right. She wore a black leather corset with a sheer skirt of black muslin, her mask also in place, but her words were stilted, and the swing of the riding crop in her hand was distracted rather than sure.

"Are you going to stay for a while, Devil?" asked one of the men, with a gratified smile. "I know my wife would greatly enjoy performing for you, wouldn't you, sweet?"

The woman curled at the man's feet looked up at her husband adoringly as he stroked her hair, her own smile eager excitement. "If it pleases you."

"I will stay, yes," said Devil, settling himself onto an empty chaise and scanning the room.

Some of the other women lounged on the floor, some were cuddled on their husband's lap. Two had collars, several more had jewel-studded anklets. But they all wore the same look of contented anticipation; secure in a world of loving care and ownership, knowing their specific sexual needs would be met, and utterly aroused at the thought of what was to come.

Pure jealousy seared him, only fueling his anger.

Charlie hesitated until he gave her a stern look, not as friend to friend, but employer to employee.

"Master Devil," she said grimly. "With your permission, we shall proceed."

"Granted."

Immediately the play began.

One woman knelt between her husband's thighs, sucking his cock while he crooned endearments. Another lady writhed in delight when her master tormented her nipples and clit with the tip of a peacock feather. Some used leather restraints, others riding crops or toys. But the couple he couldn't take his eyes off was making use of candle wax and champagne, the man drizzling a little wax on his lover's body then pouring champagne over her and himself and instructing her to lick him clean.

"Devil, my lady would be honored if you personally secured her restraints."

"Devil, would you care to pour some wax?"

"Devil, we'd certainly appreciate it if you showed us how you wield a crop."

The offers flew like arrows from around the room. Slowly he rose to his feet, bracing himself for what he was about to do. Desperate to silence the loud voice in his head protesting the wrongness. Desperate to drown out the grateful moans of pain, the effusive thanks, the orgasmic cries of the women, and instead focus on the power and control of the men.

He could do this.

Somehow.

Chapter Three

Even though she'd nearly worn a hole in the Aubusson rug, Eliza continued to pace the chamber.

Where on earth was Grayson?

Both his office and Charlotte's chamber were empty; she'd sent a maid to look. Although after her completely unladylike eruption at the chapel, it was no wonder her husband was avoiding her. Painful as it was to admit, her mother had proven right. Sweetness, obedience, and calm decorum won the day.

She had failed yet again.

After splashing some water on her face and patting it dry, Eliza scooped up a shawl and left the chamber. If Grayson was anywhere in the building, she would find him, even if she had to check every blasted room.

A half hour later she found herself in the foyer, staring uncertainly at the huge oak double doors that led into the pleasure club proper. During the few months she'd lived at Fallen, she had ventured inside on several occasions. But that seemed like more than a lifetime ago.

"Lady Eliza? Are you all right, madam?"

Nearly shrieking in surprise, Eliza stared up at Diaz. He'd always been unfailingly polite and deferential, but he was built like a mountain and moved as soundlessly as a panther. What the attractive but scarred Spaniard had done before he became butler and overseer of security at Fallen, she wasn't certain she wanted to know. "Oh, good evening, Diaz. I'm looking for my husband. Have you seen him by chance?"

The butler's eyes briefly closed, as if he were in pain. "Not for a while, madam."

Her gaze narrowed. "Where is he? In there?"

"I believe he is in one of the special activity rooms along with Miss Charlotte and some others, yes."

Eliza gasped. *Special activity rooms.* The chambers where small groups with very particular shared desires met to indulge them. Questions pounded her mind—which room? What kind of sexual play was he currently involved in? But this was greatly overshadowed by terrible jealousy. Even now, Charlotte or some other woman—or *women*—could be touching Grayson. Pleasuring him. Making him come…

"Lady Eliza?"

She blinked, her cheeks burning at the realization the odd sound echoing through the foyer had been her foot stomping. Oh, this was ludicrous. There truly wasn't any hope for her in the sweet decorum stakes. "I, er, need to go and find Lord Grayson."

"Indeed, madam. For his lordship's sake. And…the lady's."

Frowning, she reached out and touched his sleeve. "What do you mean, the lady's? You're talking about Charlotte? You don't approve of them together?"

For just an instant, his dark eyes reflected an aching sadness. Then his expression returned to its usual impassiveness. "Not for me to approve or disapprove. Forgive me, I forgot myself for a moment."

"Well. I'm going in. And if anyone attempts to stop me, I'll, er, crush their toes to powder."

"Duly noted," he said gravely. "Would you like a mask?"

Eliza smiled in gratitude. The man truly was a treasure. Only Sin, Grayson, Vice, and now Sin's wife Grace went without masks, as established owners of the club. Her status was far too precarious at present; to walk into Fallen sans mask would be foolish and risky in the extreme.

"I would."

"Then allow me to assist."

The butler took out a black and white satin demi-mask from his jacket pocket, fitted it to her face, and swiftly tugged the ribbons over her ears before tying a tight bow at the nape of her neck. Heavens. How strange, viewing the world in such a manner. Her eyesight wasn't impeded in any way, and yet knowing she was unrecognizable apart from her hair and cheeks and lips, felt so…freeing.

"Thank you."

Diaz bowed. "A pleasure, madam. Good luck," he finished, opening the door and waving her through.

It was like stepping into another world. More lavish than a palace, louder than Vauxhall Gardens with laughter and chatter, the clink of champagne glasses and melodious tunes of an expert orchestra. Not to mention the sheer number of elegantly dressed and bejeweled people. Not just men and women dancing and kissing and touching, but women and women, and men and men. This was the essence of Fallen, a sanctuary of pleasure for all.

Her courage nearly failing her, Eliza took a deep breath.

"Darling Lady Eliza, what the bloody hell are you doing in here?"

Relieved beyond measure, she turned to a welcome sight—Lord Iain Vissen, only known as Vice. The Scottish viscount was dressed to the hilt as a rather scandalous

Highland chieftain, wearing a soft wool plaid short kilt, an elaborate silver sporran, and a fine linen shirt open to reveal his broad chest. He was bare legged, barefoot, and his shoulder-length auburn hair hung loosely around his face. But instead of looking carefree, he gazed at her with real concern.

"Er, how did you know it was me, my lord?"

"Gaelic hair, lass. I see it in the looking glass and recognize it at a hundred paces."

She rolled her eyes at her own foolishness. As if a head of hair like hers ever went unnoticed. "Of course. I'm looking for Grayson."

"Thank God. He's been in that room too long already. Sin and I are at our wits' end with him. Dev is an expert, but the price he pays is far too high. And the aftermath is ugly."

"What? What are you talking about?"

Vice grimaced. "The bloody idiot thinks we don't know he has certain needs. We always played along, hoping one day Dev would be comfortable enough to be his true self. Especially when he met you...but he is a fucking dark and rigid Sassenach. Er, a most proper gentleman. Now what I want to know is, if you're going to fight for him, like the warrior we thought you were, or run away again."

Shocked to the core, she stared at the viscount. But there wasn't a trace of usual sardonic humor on his rugged face. "I...I...I want to fight."

"Good lass," said Vice, with a short, approving nod. "Then I'll take you to the room."

"At once, please," she replied, anxiety twisting her stomach into a hard knot. First Diaz, now Vice, speaking more freely to her than they ever had, and it felt like she stood on the edge of a knowledge abyss. It couldn't be clearer that Grayson's truth would change everything, and she wanted to discover exactly what that truth was. Right blasted now.

"Come this way, then," said Vice, taking her arm and

leading her out of the ballroom and down a more narrow hallway. At the end, he pointed at a closed door. "He's in there. Do you want me to accompany you?"

Eliza shook her head. "No. You carry on. I know you have much to oversee. Besides, that outrageous costume is distracting."

He grinned, lifted her hand and kissed it, then turned and hurried away.

Taking another deep breath, her heart pounding so hard it would surely burst from her chest, Eliza carefully pushed open the door and peeked in.

Oh God.

Grayson stood in the center of the room, a riding crop in one hand and a lit candlestick in the other. Several men were seated in a row, each with a woman on their lap, while two more women knelt at her husband's feet. The air was thick with the scent of arousal and pleasure, and even from here she could see the glistening, swollen cores of the women, the bright pink marks decorating their skin, their beaming faces.

But there was something desperately wrong with the scene.

In direct contrast to the elation of the others, her husband looked hellish. Parchment pale. Linen shirt damp with sweat, his mouth twisted in agonized stoicism, his beautiful green eyes haunted, glazed and red-rimmed as if trapped in a nightmare.

Horrified, Eliza stumbled into the room. "No more."

"Lady Eliza," said a low female voice to her right, the sudden grip on her wrist firm.

Even though the woman wore a mask, she knew exactly who it was, and hated her even more. "Let me go, *Mrs. Lewis.* You say you love him. And yet you witness *this* and do nothing?"

Charlotte winced. "Here, Dev is my employer, the man

who ensures the kind of security and comfort I could never have achieved alone. Do you think I enjoy watching him drink to the edge of oblivion and destroy himself?"

"Well it won't be carrying on. Not one moment. I'm taking him away," she hissed fiercely, and to her disbelief, Charlotte smiled and squeezed her hand with true warmth.

"Of course. I'll finish here."

Thankfully the other people in the room, whoever they were, didn't protest as she marched past them and slid an arm around Grayson's waist.

He blinked slowly at her, as if coming out of a deep trance. "Eliza?"

Pulling his head down and standing on her tiptoes, she whispered in his ear, "You are coming with me. Right now. Charlotte will continue on your behalf."

Grayson nodded. "I don't…I don't feel well."

"I know," Eliza whispered, then she turned to her curious audience. "Terribly sorry, my dears, but I must steal Devil away from your party. A certain portly gentleman with a rather extravagant jeweled cravat is positively *insisting* to be joined for brandy and cheroots."

One of the men laughed. "Couldn't imagine who that might be, Devil, poor chap."

"One does what one must," said Grayson, setting down the riding crop and candlestick on a nearby bench as they left the chamber. "Good evening, all."

His steps faltered halfway down the hallway. As they rounded the first corner, Eliza barely managed to maneuver him against the wall before his head dropped, and with a brandy-scented sigh, he slid to the floor.

• • •

"Grayson. Look at me. Please, please look at me."

The feminine voice sounded far away, yet very insistent. He would obey, too, but for the damned anvil pounding his skull, and he'd eaten a pound of sand if his desert-dry mouth was any indication.

"Grayson. You look at me this minute!"

He blinked terribly heavy eyelids until his wife came into focus. "I live to serve, my dear…I'm on the ground."

"You gave me such a fright," said Eliza sternly, but her eyes were wide with worry. And the way her fingers were stroking his hair was so warm and soothing, he wanted to lean into her touch, until every memory of the past few hours had been caressed away.

"Not my finest hour."

"Rather an understatement. I'm informed by members of the harem that before you went into that blasted club room, you drank nearly three bottles of brandy on an empty stomach."

"Bloody turncoats. I hope you told them I'm cancelling Christmas."

"Tell them yourself. But right now we are going upstairs and you are going to have a hot bath and eat until you are fit to burst."

"I'm not cold."

"Then why are you shivering? Everyone in Portman Square can hear your teeth chattering."

Frowning, he peered down at his hands. Damned if they weren't moving all by themselves. Actually, he was freezing. The kind of bone-deep chill that robbed a person of reason and direction. "I do feel a trifle off. Foggy, even."

"Can you get up? I'd rather we were in our chamber than this hallway. If Prinny sees, the news will be across London within the hour."

"I doubt it," he replied, but he eased to his feet anyway. Fuck, he was as unsteady as a newborn colt. "The prince owes me money, so he is neatly avoiding me right now."

"Everyone owes you money, Grayson," she said with a laugh, sliding a soft arm around his waist, the care and comfort of the action constricting his throat. "If I recall correctly, you hold promissory notes from half the *ton*."

"Maybe not quite that many. There are some aristocrats who pay their bills on time and don't crawl to me, cap in hand, for a loan or debt forgiveness. The rest are bloody leeches, want, want, want, and they demand with such entitlement," he said woodenly, barely able to suppress a wave of nausea at the never ending list of people who courted him for no other reason than financial gain. "At least Sin, Vice, Diaz, and Charlie are true. And you. My wife."

Eliza stumbled but quickly righted herself. "Sorry. New slippers. Haven't quite broken them in yet."

His chamber was deliciously warm thanks to a roaring fire in the grate. Devil sighed in relief as three footmen filled a large copper tub with buckets of steaming hot water before swiftly leaving.

Devil hauled off his clammy, sweat-soaked shirt and tossed it aside, along with his boots and trousers, then climbed into the tub. The temperature near scalded him and, as if a curtain had been yanked back, every single excruciating moment he'd been in the activity room flooded his mind. Fuck. That had been the worst night yet. Usually he could will his mind away while he played at being an alpha, but in that room, every moan and whimper, every flick and slap of leather or drop of candle wax on flesh, had sliced his soul. The women around him had come again and again, their nipples rock hard, their pussies slick with juice, and he'd been in purgatory.

A soft cloth glided across his back, and he shuddered. "Thank you," he said awkwardly into the heavy silence. "For downstairs, I mean. I wasn't really enjoying myself."

Eliza lathered the cloth with more soap and scrubbed his

arms. "A mild understatement, Grayson. You hated it. It was the most distressing thing I've ever seen. Fallen is supposed to be about pleasure for everyone, but you were gaining nothing from what you were doing. Nothing at all. Why do such a thing if it makes you hate yourself?"

Devil froze.

Well, if that wasn't the thousand-guinea question.

"I just wasn't feeling well, that's all. Far too much brandy on an empty stomach, as you noted." The lie burned his tongue.

"Poppycock."

"Eliza, I have a reputation to uphold. And to do that, sometimes I must do things I don't enjoy to ensure that reputation stays intact. All right?"

"No, it is not all right," she said angrily, tossing the cloth away. "Something that you have to drink three bottles of brandy to endure, and loathe every minute of, is not all right in any way."

Abruptly, Devil rose from the copper tub, sending a splash of water over one side. "And what would you have me do? Apart from send away a very dear friend?"

"If she truly was your friend, she wouldn't stand for you hurting yourself. Not ever. You aren't to do that again, Grayson. I'll tell Diaz and Sin and Vice to bar you from that room."

Stepping out of the tub, he stalked toward her. "Oh will you now, madam wife?"

"Count on it," Eliza snapped, hands on hips, her eyes shooting silver sparks at him. She was so magnificent in her fury on his behalf, his cock began to stiffen.

It should have been impossible after the wedding, the bottles of brandy, the evening at Fallen, and a complete lack of food, but the damned thing kept getting harder. Thickening and lengthening and sticking out from its nest of coarse black hair like a sword, while she watched. Avidly. Which only aroused him more. "Excuse me, I'll just get a towel."

"No."

The whispered word floated across the chamber, but had the impact of a shout. He stilled, helplessly obedient, his hands at his sides as he waited for her next move. Seconds later, Eliza rubbed and patted a soft yet slightly abrasive towel across his shoulders, down his back, around his backside and farther down each leg until half his body was completely dry, the other half still dripping wet.

By the time she moved around to face him, he was near panting. Agonizingly slowly, she dried his face, then his neck, dancing with a light touch across his collarbone, then rougher across his chest. Back and forth she rubbed, stimulating his chest hair and nipples with the towel until his whole upper body tingled.

He groaned, his cock so hard it nearly rested on his belly now. "Eliza…"

His wife ignored the entreaty, instead kneeling down to dry his feet and the front of his legs, sliding up from ankle to knee to thigh, circling higher and higher to pat dry his abdomen but deliberately not touching his cock. "I'm nearly done."

Devil stared down at her, a fiery angel who might have been at his feet but remained in total control, and there was only one heartfelt word he could say. "*Please*."

She smiled. And dropped the towel.

The next touch he felt was a warm, wet tongue. Licking the length of him from base to tip, then lapping the engorged head, removing the bathwater but inviting a trickle of pre-come to drip into her mouth. He moaned at the exquisite teasing of her lips and tongue, reveled in the firm grip of her fingers, hard enough to make his back arch in ecstasy. Somehow he fought the rapidly building climax, never wanting her luscious ministrations to end. Until she looked him straight in the eye and said, "Come for me. Now."

Surrendering immediately with a low, guttural roar, he climaxed. But she didn't turn away or draw back; instead she opened her mouth wider and took him deeper down her throat, greedily swallowing his seed. Finally, when the last splendid, wracking spasm had waned, and the likelihood of him passing out again was strong, he could only look at her in awe.

"Lizzie…" he breathed, not even sure he still possessed the ability to speak in complete sentences.

She stood, her lips curving into a smile so wicked his spent cock still managed to twitch. "Supper time, Grayson. You'll need your strength for the rest of the evening."

Incredulous joy battled innate caution.

Dare he hope that courtship Eliza had returned to stay?

• • •

While Grayson devoured the supper sent up on a tray, Eliza stared at the roaring fire. How could her body still be in one piece when her thoughts were flying in a thousand directions?

Exactly what had possessed her to behave how she imagined Charlotte might during one of her performances, she couldn't say. But what a result. Even now, she could still taste his salty sweetness in her mouth, and though she'd been the one kneeling, not once had she thought herself the supplicant. It had been so very heady, touching him, stroking him, teasing him to the point of madness in the guise of drying, then ordering him to come. Never had she felt so powerful, so alluring, so utterly feminine, and yet she hadn't obeyed a single Brimley teaching.

That was the difficulty, comparing the two realities of this chamber and a lifetime of instruction and rules.

Strong arms slid around her waist, the cool quilted satin of his untied black robe a delicious contrast to his hot skin. "What are you thinking about?"

"Everything and nothing," she replied with a sigh, leaning back against Grayson's bare chest. "It is very strange when a hidden truth is suddenly clear."

He froze. "And what hidden truth might that be?"

"You like me better when I am not what I ought to be."

A laugh rumbled in his chest, the tension leaving his muscles. "That is half-true. I like you *most* when you are the fiery, whip-smart angel who charges in to save me from myself, and makes her needs and desires plain."

Heat sizzled along every nerve ending. "So if I were to, for instance...tell you to do something to me, would you do it?"

Grayson's lips trailed a path of fire to her ear. "Anything that brought you pleasure, yes."

"Then undress me."

His intake of breath was audible, even over the crackle and snap of the fire, and Eliza shivered in excitement. When she lifted her arms, he tugged off her gown with deliberate care and draped it over the low side table. Then he got to work on her stays, loosening the silken cords, every scrape and chuff only increasing her anticipation as the constricting garment gaped a little farther with each tug and pull. Last of all he removed her knee-length chemise, though accidentally tearing it from her body might have been a better description. He now stared in comical dismay at the two jagged halves of whisper-thin linen in his hands.

"I'll buy you a new one. No, twenty."

Eliza laughed, sinking onto the long chaise next to the fire. "My, my. The ledgers will never recover. Now, perhaps you should pour me a drink. There was a bottle of champagne on that dinner tray, wasn't there?"

In record time, Grayson brought over two full glasses of champagne, but as he returned, his toes caught in the braid of the rug and he stumbled, sending an arc of golden, fizzing liquid across her breasts and belly. "Shit. I'm sorry, Eliza, I'll get a cloth—"

"No," she said softly. "I think your tongue would do a better job."

Wordlessly, his hot gaze dancing over her naked, champagne-soaked body, Grayson sank to his knees next to the chaise. He started with her collarbone, collecting the drips before licking down the outer curves of her breasts. His mouth was warm and wet, his tongue a smooth delight on her skin, and yet every so often his teeth grazed her, making her whimper.

Her nipples hardened painfully, begging to be sucked without delay, but he took his time circling the areola with the tips of his fingers. She let him, knowing in a flurry of anticipation that he wouldn't stop this time, not even if they had an audience of thousands. Knowing he prepared her for an orgasm the likes of which she had never experienced.

When Grayson's tongue lashed her nipple, she squirmed with desire. Finally his hard lips engulfed the taut peak and drew firmly, over and over, sending fierce jolts of pleasure to her liquid, throbbing core.

"More?" he whispered. "I could suck your nipples for hours, you know."

Eliza inhaled unsteadily. "It feels so good, but I need your mouth between my legs. I want…I want you to lick my pussy."

Shock widened his eyes at the word he often used but she never had. Then he smiled, a smile so tender and wicked, she nearly came on the spot when his big, strong hands carefully spread her thighs wide and he lowered his head.

His thumbs parted the thatch of auburn curls guarding her mound, and for a brief moment, his breath was a gentle tease against her soaked flesh. Then his tongue drove in, strong and sure and rough, licking her folds and massaging her clit until she came with a low scream. But Grayson didn't stop as the pulses rocked her entire body, just kept greedily lapping up the juice as it trickled from her center, even pushing his tongue deep inside her for more. When he lightly pinched her clit with his thumb and forefinger while his tongue ruthlessly plundered, she came again, her hips bucking wildly.

"Yes, Lizzie," he panted against her. "Keep coming in my mouth. Your pussy tastes so good."

Eliza shook her head, her body wrung out from the power of her orgasms, and yet wanting more. Needing to be filled.

Leaning forward, she took the lapels of Grayson's robe in her hands, tugging him upward until his mouth was level with hers. Then she kissed him, savoring the sweet and musky taste of champagne and wetness he'd drank from her, while one hand slid down to find his thick cock beautifully, wonderfully hard and ready.

"Excellent," she purred, giving his erection a firm squeeze. "Now I'm going to ride you, and we'll test exactly how well-made this chaise really is."

"Yes. Fuck, yes," said Grayson hoarsely, quickly settling himself on the chaise, one long leg resting against the back, the other braced on the floor. When she slowly sank down onto his engorged cock, he groaned, his eyes closing briefly in an expression of total erotic bliss. Her heart clenched at the thought of how many moments she'd missed listening to her head rather than her intuition. But there was no time to dwell on that now, not when her neglected body was so desperate to feel him deep.

Their rhythm remained awkward at first as she bore down and he thrust upward, but after several strokes they were gorgeously, perfectly together, straining and grinding and gasping as they hurtled toward ecstasy. Then Grayson pressed her clit with his thumb and she tumbled over the edge, her inner muscles pulsing and clenching him so hard he jerked and spurted long streams of hot seed inside her.

Exhausted, she sighed with happiness and collapsed onto his chest. His arms immediately closed around her, and when one hand began stroking her back, she only had time to process one last thought before the sleep of the utterly sated overcame her.

Thank heavens the chaise was sturdier than it looked.

Chapter Four

"Stop it, the pair of you. Fucking married men. This is a serious business meeting, and you both keep staring at the bloody door like you want to escape. You're both goddamned crazy. Grace and Eliza are just women. Perfectly nice women, I grant you, but not goddesses!"

Devil raised an eyebrow at Vice's irritable outburst, but it was difficult to manufacture a more scathing response when he felt so damned calm and content. Two days had passed since Sin and Grace's wedding and the awful evening at the club which had turned into the best night of his life. For the first time in months, he was starting to feel…hope. He and Eliza were talking, really talking, she was back where she belonged with him in the office, and the sex just kept getting better. He'd been a fool to doubt the reason she had returned. "On the contrary. Eliza is absolutely a goddess, and your blathering is preventing me from joining her in my office. We have piles of accounts to go through."

"You know, Dev," said Sin with a smirk, "the harem reports the oddest sounds coming from your office when you and Eliza are working on all those accounts."

Devil's lips twitched. "No idea what you're talking about. But I might counter with the mysterious orders for jade dildos and quantities of scented oil that somehow never make it to the toy chamber."

His friend coughed and looked away.

"My God," exclaimed Vice, slapping the table. "Look at his cheeks! Never thought I'd see the day the legendary Sebastian St. John blushed like a fucking debutante. I rest my case, marriage has destroyed him. Both of you should hand over your shares to me and retire to Bath with all the other feeble ancients."

Sin shook his head. "One day, dear boy, one day, you'll find the woman who turns your life upside down in the best way. God knows the level of hellion she'd have to be to make waves in your world, though. London might never recover."

"Which is exactly why I shall never succumb," said Vice, shuddering. "But can we please, *please* return to the matter at hand? Midsummer Night's festivities? The date is only a week away now, and I have preparations to oversee."

Devil sat back on his chair, tapping his chin. "I wondered about, ah, pagan."

"Pagan? Fairies and fire and roses and such? Hmmm, yes. A sterling choice for those of us with majestic red h...oh Christ."

"What?"

"I thought you were being creative and out of the ledger for once, but you just want to show off your wife. Bastard."

"Keep talking," said Devil, floundering for a plausible diversion from his fanciful idea. "That Lowlands accent is so very charming."

"*Lowlands?* Why, you—"

"Gentlemen," drawled Sin. "And I use that term in the loosest possible sense. If we are going pagan, Madame Alice will want to know as soon as possible the kind of costumes everyone will want. Plenty of silks and satins in shades of red, gold, topaz, amber…"

"I will, of course, be the Midsummer Night king," said Vice, his eyes glinting. "Just imagine the hedonism. It may even out-scandal the pirate ball. Although, er, with no kidnappings or shootings, naturally."

Devil rolled his eyes. "I doubt Sin, or Grace for that matter, ever wish to be reminded of that night, you numbskull. But a pagan ball it is. We can begin hiring extra staff and preparing orders for Madame Alice, the florists, and merchants this afternoon. Now, if you'll both excuse me, I promised Eliza I'd escort her to Mayfair for some shopping."

Sin and Vice both stared at him as if he'd grown another head.

"Shopping?" said Sin dubiously. "Do you even know what a shop looks like?"

"Make sure you take plenty of money," added Vice. "They usually don't expect aristocrats to pay on the day, but might make an exception for you when your lackluster people skills run out and the ice man appeareth…hmmm, Grayson and Eliza, ice and fire. Now that is poetry. I am actually a genius in all ways; no wonder I outrank you both."

"Poor deluded Scot," said Devil, rising from his chair.

"Letting them win the odd battle for morale really was a mistake," said Sin gravely.

His shoulders shaking with silent laughter, Devil escaped from the room before Vice's threatened head explosion occurred. The accounts office was just three doors along from their combined office, so fortunately he didn't have far to go to collect Eliza.

Poking his head around the door, he watched her frown and peer at a ledger then make a note on a fresh sheet of paper.

"Do we need matching spectacles, madam wife?"

She snorted. "No, my lord husband, you just need to learn how to use a pen. Good heavens, your handwriting hasn't improved a jot."

"Well, I can't be perfect in *every* way."

"Quite. That would be dreary."

Devil ambled into the room and kicked the door shut behind him. "Eliza Jean Brimley Deveraux, do I detect a hint of sarcasm in your tone?"

"Only a hint?" said Eliza, her lips twitching. "One of us is losing our touch. Actually, I think it is me. I've been trying to solve a mystery in this ledger for hours now and it is driving me quite batty."

"Oh? What is it?"

"Every month, a certain sum is paid to a creditor by the name of Christian Holdings. But no invoices come in, nor do notes for goods supplied. It's like the money just disappears into thin air. And it's not a small sum; it is a thousand guineas each month!"

He leaned against the side of the desk and sighed. "Don't worry about that money. It is a, ah, personal expense of mine."

Eliza gripped the pen so hard her knuckles whitened. "A personal expense such as?"

"It isn't important, really."

"You have a child, don't you? A son called Christian. How old is he? Please don't say he's a baby, I…"

Devil laughed at the sheer ludicrousness of the words. Clearly he'd concealed his vampire monk identity better than even he thought. Just as quickly he halted, his cheeks heating in shame at the hurt look on Eliza's face. Damnation. She really didn't know.

"There is no child, Eliza. God no…" he began, and then for some unknown reason, the words just whooshed out in a breath. "The name in the ledger isn't Christian Holdings,

it is Christina Hemmings. That is my mother's maiden name.
I set up a private account through my bankers so she would
never go without, and she picks up the purse each month
from them. Mother thinks Reyburn provides her allowance,
but that useless fucking bastard couldn't stump for a street
pie seller, let alone a marchioness. He doesn't have a feather
to fly with."

"What? But he is always out. The opera…the parties and
horses…all the scandal sheets positively gush over his and
your brother's comings and goings."

Devil gripped the edge of the desk so he wouldn't pick
something up and hurl it at the wall. "A complete facade.
My bankers did some discreet investigating, and it seems his
creditors are no longer blinded by the title. They are circling
now, and it is going to be messy. My brother will have nothing
to inherit at this rate. Reyburn cares nothing for those he
bankrupts because he never pays his bills, so he'll be shown no
mercy in return. Fucking peers. Those who steal from others
deserve everything they get."

"And yet you…you help your mother."

"Not really," he said, attempting a smile. "The servants'
wages get paid from that money. I won't have fifty maids and
footmen and gardeners, or their families, starving because of
my scapegrace father."

Eliza didn't smile back. "Oh, Grayson," she said softly.
"What really happened between you and him?"

Rage and pain surged and twisted through his body, so
powerful he shoved himself away from the desk and crossed
the office to stare blankly out the window. "Nothing worth
repeating. But it is a bridge that is well and truly burned, and
I have no desire whatsoever to reconcile. Shall we go? I feel a
desperate need for some fresh air."

"Grayson…"

He didn't turn around. Maybe in the future he might

speak of the time Reyburn and his valet had nearly killed him "to make a man out of him" after his submissive tendencies had come to light.

But that day was not today.

· · ·

So much pain.

Staring at her husband's rigid back, Eliza attempted to swallow the barrage of questions on the tip of her tongue. Whatever happened might have been years ago, but it had to be far worse than she imagined for the bitter estrangement to continue so long. Grayson had rarely talked about his father during their marriage, and Lord and Lady Reyburn hadn't attended their wedding. Back then, Grayson explained away their absence with an expensive wedding gift and an apology note stating they were in Italy.

"They were here, weren't they. Your parents," she said slowly. "Did they choose not to attend our wedding, or did you not invite them?"

It shouldn't have been possible, but Grayson tensed further. Then he let out an audible breath. "I invited my brother; he refused. I didn't invite my parents. But they wouldn't have come even if I had. We haven't spoken in nearly ten years."

Shocked to the core, she couldn't muffle a gasp. Ten *years*?

Nearly sprinting across the room, Eliza wound her arms around his waist and rested her cheek against his back. His lean, muscular form felt like a statue against her and, dismayed, she began stroking his chest. "It must have been something awful."

Abruptly, he turned in her arms, his green eyes glittering. "Don't push me, Eliza."

She hesitated, weighing the words against the challenge,

the naked plea in his gaze. "Ten years ago you would have been at Cambridge, mastering mathematics. Learning about the world. And…yourself. Was university where you discovered your preference for a woman being in control?"

"I…fuck. Perhaps. Can't we save this for another time?"

"No," Eliza said, lifting her hand to cup his cheek. Then, on a moment of impulse, she threaded her fingers through his short-cropped hair and tugged firmly on the silken strands.

Grayson moaned, the sound so intensely sexual that moisture gathered between her legs. "You're going to make me tell you, aren't you?"

"Yes, darling, I am," she replied in the steeliest tone she could muster, the relaxing of his shoulders and stark relief in his eyes giving her the courage to add: "Because I am in charge here. I'll have it the way I like it. But first, I want you to kiss me."

Her husband's lips crashed down onto hers, not with cool finesse but raw hunger, as though the darkness that had been suppressed for so long was finally bursting free. Then his arms closed around her waist like steel bars, and he lifted and pressed her against the office wall, spreading her thighs and wrapping them around his hips. The wall was chilly and unforgiving against her back, but she didn't break the scorching kiss, just held him tightly and continued to stroke and tug at his hair. This could be it. The moment that defined whether their marriage might succeed or fail. And she wanted it to succeed more than anything in the world.

Eventually Eliza leaned forward, scraping her teeth along his earlobe and biting down ever so slightly, just enough to leave a small imprint. Grayson still didn't speak, but his engorged cock jerked against her mound, and when she slid her free hand between them and unfastened his trousers, the head of his erection spilled out, wet with pre-come.

"Now you may answer me, Grayson," she said softly but

sternly, curling her fingers around his cock and caressing him.

He shuddered. "God. Please let me come."

"I want to. I want to so badly, darling. My pussy is wet and aching, and I know you will fill me so very full. I love it when you are deep inside me. But you are holding on to a terrible hurt right now, and I *cannot allow* that between us."

Gasping, he nuzzled into the side of her neck, his lips hard and smooth, his jaw slightly scratchy. "What do you want to know, Eliza? The friends I didn't make because I hated the usual lordly pursuits of hunting and shooting? The rumors that started about me because I didn't go into the village and fuck every woman I saw or leave a trail of bastards in my wake?"

"Yes, that's it," she crooned, holding him close as the words spilled out. "Very good. What else?"

"I tried. Fuck, I tried. But the women were so…so deferential. They were in awe of my father's title, and mine, even though it is just a courtesy one. They wanted to serve and be owned and ordered about by me."

"And you didn't want that at all," she said, squeezing the base of his erection in reward.

He panted, arching his back slightly so his cock pressed harder against her fingers. "No. Then one day I met Charlie. She hosted parties you see, for men, ah, exploring. Some enjoyed both male and female lovers, some just male. But a few of us were gifted the opportunity to learn about submission."

Ignoring the sharp twinge at the mention of Charlotte, too proud and relieved that Grayson was finally sharing these deeply personal memories, Eliza shifted so the head of his cock rubbed against her swollen, wet labia. "I am very pleased with you. I know it is hard to share the times you don't wish to speak of, but it makes me admire you more, my brave darling. Now you are going to make me scream and fill my pussy with come. I want every drop you have."

He kissed her cheek, then in one lightning fast movement, he fitted his cock to her sheath and drove deep. They both moaned at the friction, the sheer bliss as her inner walls clamped around his length, holding him inside her. Grayson's mouth trailed down her neck and across the tops of her breasts as he thrust and withdrew, grinding his hips against her, the wall ensuring she didn't have to do anything but wrap her legs tighter around his waist to bring him even closer.

"Lizzie," he groaned, reaching down to tease her clit. "Fuck, you're so wet and hot. Fucking heaven. So smart and fiery and beautiful…"

The orgasm exploded and she screamed his name, her fingernails shredding his linen shirt as she bucked and writhed. Seconds later Grayson rammed deep inside her and came with a guttural cry, every long, hot spurt of his seed like a sensual lash inside her.

"Oh dear," she said dreamily, as he stepped back from the wall and walked unsteadily across the room toward the huge, padded desk chair, every step pushing and pulling his cock against her tender channel until she quivered.

"What's wrong?" he said as he carefully sat down in the chair and held her close.

"I've already sent four chemises to the rag bag this week, you rogue, and I do believe I'll be sending a fifth after today."

He grinned. "Hardly my fault they don't make chemises like they used to. But when you decide to let me up, we'll make our way to Mayfair. Actually, you're not the only one who'll be sending something to the rag bag today. My shirt has gone to that great dressing room in the sky, but it would like you to know it accepted its demise with a merry heart…ow. Eliza Jean Brimley Deveraux, did you just pinch your poor, innocent husband…ow. Seriously, my dear, if you keep that up I'm going to get hard again."

Eliza's tongue darted out and licked his lips. "Exactly how is that a problem?"

"I don't know. What were we talking about again?"

"An urgent need for Mayfair."

"The shops can wait," said Grayson, rocking her on his lap and making her whimper.

"Yes," she agreed, cupping his face in her hands for a long, carnal kiss, "they can."

. . .

"Grayson, you are staring at me."

"Not exactly," Devil murmured several hours later, as his luxurious carriage glided around a corner and sped toward Mayfair. "I'm imagining you as Queen of the Fairies. Gold and diamond tiara, watered green silk tunic, and some roses. Definitely no chemise or stays."

"So the three of you have decided on the Midsummer Night ball theme, then?"

"I believe so. Madame Alice will visit to measure you for your costume and show you a range of fabrics, but with that glorious hair, I would humbly beg you to choose a shade of green."

"Humbly?" she said with a raised eyebrow.

He widened his eyes, innocent as a choirboy. "I am more than willing to get on my knees."

"Hmmm. Agreeable things do occur when you are there. I'll consider your request, although I'm not sure about the 'no stays' idea. My breasts are too big to run amok."

Devil sighed in delicious remembrance. "Indeed."

"Oh good grief. You're thinking of them running amok, aren't you?"

"Not at all, my dear. Ledgers. I am definitely thinking about ledgers right now."

"What you should be thinking of is your own costume," said Eliza, sitting forward on the leather carriage squab. "If I am to be queen, will you be king?"

"Vice would shoot me on the spot if I attempted to usurp his throne. I'll wear whatever costume you think best. Although please don't make me be a bloody tree. Or part of a Stonehenge display. It's not my fault my genius manifests itself in ways other than waltzing. Or penmanship. Or carrying drinks."

"Oh, I think you have the odd talent to make up for it. And you really do make ink spots look dashing."

Devil laughed, his head falling back on the squab in a movement of utter relaxation. It was an odd feeling. His body probably didn't know which way was up, as he slept and ate and worked and made love to his spouse like a normal person. But this morning had been another significant step forward, when he'd spoken for the first time of his Cambridge days and Charlotte's parties.

The confession had been easier than expected, and that was entirely because of the way Eliza had coaxed and praised and gently ordered him. But hell, it already felt like a burden had been lifted from his shoulders. She hadn't run or gotten angry or frightened, just led him into several exquisitely powerful climaxes. Again, but far stronger than before, hope rose. Hope that in time he could tell her everything, even his darkest secrets.

When the carriage eventually came to a halt in Cavendish Square, he and Eliza stepped out onto the footpath. It was a beautiful day to be outdoors, clear and warm, as they began to stroll arm in arm through the heart of Mayfair.

Eliza tilted her head back so the sun could reach under her bonnet brim. "This is lovely."

"Where do you want to go? Do you have shops you prefer? I'm afraid I have no bloody idea when it comes to ladies' attire."

"Clark and Debenham, on Wigmore Street," she replied. "I haven't been there in an age, but the quality is excellent."

"Even better. We're practically there. In the work of a moment, you shall have chemises to last at least a few weeks."

As it seemed like half of London had also ventured out to enjoy the sunshine, it actually took far longer to walk to the grand building than he'd estimated. He'd never been in the place himself, but the harem certainly spent a great deal of time and money there.

Walking up the steps and into the building was like stepping into a gigantic henhouse. It was noisy as hell and there were people everywhere, mostly women and children, but also the odd gentleman and plenty of footmen lugging hat and garment boxes. The salesmen were easy to spot, dressed in black trousers, shirts, and waistcoats, and hurrying from one corner of the enormous shop to the other. Some carried ready-made gowns and pelisses, but most held oversized bolts of fabric in satin and twill.

Eliza's gaze darted from one side to the other, her smile bright with anticipation. "I don't even know where to start."

"Start with the chemise and work your way out to gloves," he replied, propping himself up against a pillar as Eliza bustled around him, pointing out bombazines and sarsnets, near-swooning over some Parisian fashion plates, and examining a bolt of satin the color of new leaves. The service had been adequate enough to start, but when he slipped two attendants a guinea apiece, it became positively fawning as they attempted to outsprint each other in collecting and presenting anything that took Eliza's fancy.

Unfortunately his generosity drew the attention of several well-dressed ladies, who immediately began gossiping behind their fans, their pointed gazes and knowing looks reminding him why he never ventured into town.

"Grayson! What do you think of this fabric?" said Eliza merrily, her eyes sparkling. Suddenly the old bats and boredom were worth it as she twirled around him with a bolt of sky blue-striped muslin, one hand discreetly cupping his cock as she swished past.

"Delightful. Couldn't adore it more."

She laughed, her wicked smile promising a wealth of future delights. Until the smile slipped from her face and she paled.

Devil frowned. "What's the matter? Eliza?"

"Can we leave?"

"Are you feeling unwell?"

"I'm fine," she said briskly. "Can we just leave at once, please? I'll find some fabric elsewhere for chemises and such."

Thoroughly confused at the complete change in her mood, he tucked her arm through his. "All right then, I—"

"Yoo-hoo! Lord Grayson! Eliza!" called Lady Brimley, barreling through a small crowd of people to reach them. "I didn't even believe the whispers when I heard you two were in here shopping your hearts out, but what a happy surprise. You are just the couple I wanted to find."

Eliza almost folded in on herself as her mother descended. Sure they had an uneasy relationship most of the time, and the countess could be arrogant, selfish, and a rather foolish slave to the *ton*, but his wife's reaction seemed rather excessive.

"Lady Brimley," he said politely, bowing over his mother-in-law's hand. "How may I assist?"

"Dear boy. Has Eliza spoken to you? She swore to me she would."

He glanced at his wife, who appeared to have lost even more color from her cheeks. "About what in particular?"

"Nothing," said Eliza through bloodless lips. "Mother, not now. You'll ruin everything."

Devil's gaze narrowed at the silent war of looks shooting

between his wife and her mother. What the hell was going on? "Eliza?"

Lady Brimley suddenly encircled his arm with her hand, the cloying touch both annoying and unwelcome. "My daughter might care nothing for the wellbeing of others, but I'm certain you do not feel the same, Lord Grayson. You've always been so generous and giving toward her, and that is why I feel confident approaching you for the smallest of favors."

Uneasiness settled like a wet overcoat. "I see. Perhaps we might continue this conversation in a more private setting?"

Eliza frantically shook her head, but his mother-in-law beamed. "Excellent idea. A tea shop it is."

Chapter Five

The tea was hot and sweet, and a tiered selection of tarts and cream cakes and pastries sat within arm's reach, but even a nibble would have her casting up her accounts. A carriage wreck was about to occur right before her eyes, and there wasn't a thing she could do to stop it.

Eliza watched in utter misery as her mother finished a jam tart and dabbed her mouth with a linen napkin.

"Lord Grayson," said Lady Brimley, fluttering her lashes. "While I never expected a son-in-law quite so mired in, er, trade, your social connections prove that nasty stain can be overcome. And as I said earlier, I have always admired your generosity toward my daughter. But now that generosity and giving, that caring concern, must go wider."

Grayson's expression eased. "Are you raising funds for a charity, Lady Brimley? A church or hospital or orphanage perhaps? I'd be pleased to donate if that is the case."

"Something like that, dear boy. A most worthy cause."

"Which is?" her husband said a trifle impatiently, and Eliza wanted to slide under the table.

"The Brimley Finishing Academy!"

He frowned. "I'm not sure I understand. I thought your school was well-placed financially, all those grateful families regularly contributing after a successful match, alongside all the term fees from current students."

Lady Brimley's smile thinned. "That was the case. Until my own daughter and her husband decided to live apart in a very public fashion after just a few months of marriage."

"Ah," said Grayson, clearing his throat. "I see. But surely the school's coffers could survive that? And as we are currently reconciling, that shouldn't affect the school's reputation in the future?"

"Well, yes. And I applaud every sacrifice my daughter has made to achieve that reconciliation."

Eliza clenched her fists. "I haven't made any sacrifices, Mother."

"Yes you have! Behaving like a strumpet in public just to please your husband. Oh, my dear, I saw what you did while looking at fabrics, and my heart broke for you. But rest assured that I forgive you, for it is a woman's lot to endure distasteful things. Do you think I wanted to tak...er, borrow the money? No, I did not. But I must tolerate Brimley's gross weaknesses as any good wife should."

Grayson didn't look at her, but she felt his shock and shame like a physical blow. The death knell to her fledgling happiness, delivered in a few sharp words.

"Mother," she began, her temper barely leashed now. "Our situations are completely diff—"

"No need to explain, Eliza," said Grayson icily, making her shiver. "As your mother rightly points out, it is the wife who suffers when her husband is inadequate. Tell me, Lady Brimley, how much were you compelled to *borrow* from the academy?"

"Ten thousand pounds. It made me feel ill inside, and I am

ashamed to admit I felt scorn for Brimley when he confessed. Such abhorrent weakness, a man looking to a woman for guidance and salvation. But as I said, well-bred ladies like Eliza and I, we endure."

"Indeed. I'll arrange a draft to pay the debt," he replied in a voice so dead and flat her heart pounded in warning.

"No!" she burst out. "Grayson—"

"Be quiet!" her mother hissed.

Grayson tilted his head, his eyes an emerald abyss. "I'm unsure why you protest, Eliza. I needed the reminder that for the *ton*, it is always about money. Money to pretend, money to extract from difficulty, money to risk anew. Of course you aren't any different."

"Don't, darling—"

"My lady. Please, there is no need for this, the debt will be paid and the academy will survive. Actually, I must commend your performance. And your tactics of course, the timing of the request was impeccable. Enough to ensure I heard it in a very amiable frame of mind, but not so long you couldn't stomach your unwanted duty for another minute. Now, who would like a cake or pastry? They certainly look delicious."

For the first time in her life, Lady Brimley hesitated, perhaps finally realizing all might not be well. "That is very, very kind, Lord Grayson, but I must rush to tell Brimley the good news. He'll be so relieved. I know this has weighed heavily on his mind. The man has barely slept for the past few weeks."

And with a quick smile and pat on the hand, Lady Brimley scampered out of the tea shop in a flurry of cream skirts.

The silence was agonizing, but Grayson didn't meet her gaze, just methodically dissected a raisin pastry and sipped his lemon-infused tea.

"I'm so sorry," she choked out eventually.

He stood, the scrape of the chair on the wooden floor an

even more painful sound than usual. "Hate to break up this tea party, but I've just remembered an urgent appointment I must attend. Do you wish to stay here? I'll send another carriage to fetch you later if you want to continue shopping."

Terror engulfed her. This was the Devil society whispered about: the man of ice for which money remained the only consideration, the only thing that didn't let him down. She'd shoved him back into that lonely, broken hell because she couldn't stand up to her blasted mother.

"No," Eliza said firmly, pushing back her own chair. "I'm coming with you."

Grayson ambled out of the tea shop, and when she hurried after him and curled her hand around his arm, he flinched away.

"Ah, excellent," he said, as though she was a distant acquaintance. "Coachman's managed to pull up just over there. Thought for a moment the number of people might prevent him stopping and we'd be walking all the way back to Portman Square."

"Don't be Devil and shut me out," she whispered. "At least give me a chance to explain."

"Please get into the carriage, Eliza. We've had enough public discussion for one afternoon, don't you think?"

Scrambling into the conveyance, she bit her lip until he climbed in behind her and shut the door. As soon as they were moving, she leaned forward and took his hand. "Grayson, let me—"

"There is not a single thing that needs explaining," he said, staring out the window. "It is all very clear. You came to London ostensibly for Sin and Grace's wedding, but what you really wanted was a substantial bank draft. To ensure the likelihood of this happening, you gritted your teeth and altered your personality to please your weak, pathetic husband, while performing acts of a sexual nature that you loathed and mocked and sought absolution for later."

"No," she said fiercely. "Mother talked of a situation completely different to mine. And she is so very wrong."

"You didn't come to London seeking ten thousand pounds from me, then?"

"She charged me with that task. I didn't want to, though, especially when I learned she'd stolen money from the academy. But they were facing ruin. Papa is terrible when it comes to finances. He didn't follow your excellent investing advice and lost a great deal in stocks. But he is a good man who didn't deserve to lose everything because of one mistake. What else could I do?"

"You could have asked me for the money at any time, Eliza. Instead you forced your way back into my life, working with me, dining with me, sharing my bed. You fucked me, owned me, stripped me bare and made me believe...and all the time it was about duty."

"Grayson, *no*. I've never been so happy. Never felt so... so confident and beautiful as I have in the last few days. I love instructing you...controlling your pleasure..." she said frantically, but he tugged his hand away from her hold, again staring blankly out the window.

And her heart shattered.

• • •

Fifteen thousand pounds.

Signing his name on a bank draft, Devil blew on the ink to help it dry a little faster. He'd added the extra five to cover any interest, but also to allow the Brimleys some breathing room until their next quarterly payments arrived from their various tenants and holdings.

As it turned out, while Lord Brimley had made a series of catastrophic investment decisions, he wasn't altogether clueless when it came to land improvements and crops. With proper drainage, some new equipment, and a decent steward overseeing the books, it was possible they could turn a small profit next year, and a healthy one the year after. Lady Brimley he still couldn't stomach, especially her complete lack of remorse at stealing the money from her own school, but at least she hadn't done anything like it before.

Actually, the only clueless person in this whole fucking mess was him. Duped not once but twice, by the woman he'd chosen to marry.

Fuck, it stung.

Especially after the way he'd carried on in the last few days, all happy and smug at his good fortune. No wonder Vice had wanted to punch him in the nose. At least his friend wouldn't have to now, since the fates had done the job instead. It seemed he was indeed destined for the solitary life, which was fine. He'd done it before, he could do it again. The scraped-raw, hollow feeling would lessen over time, and soon it would be gone entirely as one day of blessed numbness blended into the next.

A knock sounded on the office door.

"Come in," he called, not looking up as the door swung open. The harem had actually been very solicitous after he and Eliza returned home, somehow sensing that something had gone terribly wrong; when he'd ordered an early dinner so he might make headway on Fallen's income and expenditure for the month, a tray had been promised at once.

"Good evening, Grayson."

Very carefully, he put his pen down. "What are you doing here, Eliza?"

"Bringing you supper. I hoped…I want very much to talk to you."

Devil rubbed a hand over his face, hating the fact that his body responded to her even now. Hating the width and breadth of such a pathetic need, that he still craved time and conversation with a woman who only did things for money. "I am a little hungry. What have the kitchens sent?"

Eliza set the tray down on his desk and lifted the lid. "Roasted beef, potatoes with butter and parsley, green beans...oh Grayson, your face! You look like you've been bathing in ink."

A glance at his right hand revealed a thick smear of blue. Hell and damnation. He really needed to purchase a new pen and inkpot set. "Ah well, you won't have to worry about it much longer."

She stilled. "Won't I?"

"Surely you'll be returning to Lincolnshire shortly?"

"I have no plans to. In fact, I fear you may find me a very difficult guest to get rid of."

Devil swallowed a forkful of green beans as if savoring the fresh, delicate flavor, when instead he was stalling for time. "This is quite unnecessary, Eliza. The draft is right here. I've added an extra five thousand to last them until next quarter. You don't have to pretend anymore."

"I am *not* pretending. The last few days have been the best of my life. Working with you again, living here at Fallen...I feel useful, not drifting along. And the lovemaking, good heavens, Grayson, do you think I could fake those responses? Anyone can scream or moan or gasp, I grant you that. But what about my skin, glistening and flushed pink? My swollen, rock hard nipples?"

"Don't, Eliza," he said gruffly, concentrating on not squirming in his chair.

But she continued as if he hadn't spoken. "Not to mention my pussy. You saw and felt how wet I was. You licked that moisture up, put your tongue inside me to gather more. And when I came, I gripped your cock so tight, you always felt the pulses. I know you did, because then you filled me up with your seed. By the by, do you think we might have made a baby, Grayson? I've been thinking about it a lot. How much I would love to watch my belly grow big with your child. To hold our son or daughter in my arms."

A yearning so fierce, so powerful, he couldn't sit down a moment longer overwhelmed him, and he shoved back his chair and walked over to the floor-to-ceiling shelves crammed with hundreds of leather-bound books. "I don't know," he bit out.

"Maybe earlier today we did. I don't think you have ever taken me so hard and deep as up against that wall over there. And in the chair, oh my. Now that I know you like it when I speak forcefully, when I hold you and guide your pleasure, I will give you what you need."

"You won't," he said hoarsely, the two words tumbling out before he could halt them.

She stepped forward to grip the back of the chaise. "How…how so?"

"What we have done so far, it has been very, very good, but it is only part of what I truly need."

"Then tell me. Tell me the rest. How can I know unless you do?"

Bracing one hand on the bookshelf, he stared at Eliza, feeling like he walked a carnival tightrope. She said she wanted to know, but the truth had already destroyed him once.

"It is worse than you think," he said quietly.

"Grayson, now you are scaring me."

Rage bubbled. "Good. The sooner you realize exactly how twisted I am, the sooner you'll leave."

"*Twisted?* What on earth are you talking about?"

"I like pain, Eliza. In sexual play."

"Well, I know that. You certainly liked me tugging your hair and scratching you with my nails this morning," she said soothingly, a relieved smile playing about her lips. "And that is quite, quite fine."

"You know nothing," he snarled, angry at her calm acceptance when she didn't understand at all. "When I say I like pain, I mean I like it rough and harsh and hurting. In my last year at Eton, I used to misbehave to get the cane. The more strokes the better. And then I'd go to my room and come in my hand because I was so hard. Reyburn found out and was so furious he threatened to cut me off. I stopped for a while, but when I started Cambridge, the need returned, stronger than ever."

"And you met Charlotte."

"I did. And everything was a splendid whirl of discovery. I could be my true self. The others didn't judge me, didn't care that I liked canes and crops and clamps and cock rings. It was a happy time, until Reyburn's spies discovered why I chose to remain in the village rather than leave in the term breaks. When I finally did go home for Christmas in 1803, Reyburn and his valet were waiting."

Eliza gasped. "What did they do?"

"Beat me. But as the bard said, *therein lies the rub*. I didn't cower or scream or beg for mercy. I laughed. And after one particularly good strike with a buckled belt, I came in my trousers. Reyburn used his fists after that, until his hands became too sore and his valet stepped in. When I stopped moving, he threw me out onto the footpath in the ice and snow. The cold was enough to wake me up, and I staggered and crawled to Charlotte's townhouse. She took me in. End of story."

Deafening silence filled the office. Eliza ran across the room, but her touch on his shoulder was too much, threatening to break his fragile composure. "Grayson…"

He shook her off. "Don't. Just leave. If you care at all, leave me be."

His wife hesitated for an achingly long moment then fled, slamming the office door behind her.

Slowly, Devil slid down the bookshelf front, until he sprawled on the ground. Finally, no more pretense or lies or secrets. Now that Eliza knew the whole disgusting truth, she would leave for good. His eyes burned, his head throbbed, and his gut churned with nausea at the thought of his bleak, empty future, but he wouldn't succumb. It was far better like this.

Or at least, it would be.

· · ·

Near-blinded by her tears, Eliza ran and ran, having no idea where she was going as she sprinted down several hallways, until her feet came to a sudden halt outside Charlotte's chamber.

Without hesitating, she pounded on the door, and a minute later it opened to reveal Grayson's savior in a gold satin dressing gown, a very perplexed expression on her face.

"Charlotte," she choked out on a sob, knowing she probably looked like a complete fright. "May I come in?"

"Why?" said Charlotte in a blunt but not unfriendly tone.

"I n-need to speak with you about Grayson. He…he just told me about that night with his father. Actually he told me everything. Cambridge, the parties…"

The door swung wide. "Come in. I apologize for the mess, but I'm just getting ready for a performance."

"No need to apologize," Eliza said quickly. "I am the one who is sorry. I had no idea what you did. How you saved his life, gave him a home after Lord Reyburn…my God, that man better hope he never meets me in the street."

"The marquess is a bastard of the highest order. Dev loses nothing being estranged from him, and we'll jostle for grave-spitting position when the man finally does everyone a favor and cocks up his toes."

"What about Grayson's mother and brother?"

"His mother doesn't have a maternal bone in her body. I believe the two boys were mostly raised by governesses and tutors. But his brother, well that is a damned shame. Lord Upton is a decent fellow by all accounts."

Eliza nodded. "And you are a very decent woman. I treated you shamefully, especially at the chapel. Jealousy is a terrible thing, especially knowing you and Grayson..."

"Me and Grayson, what exactly?"

"You know," she mumbled uncomfortably, wanting to discuss her husband's previous liaisons like she wanted to be crushed by a runaway cart. "The two of you...together."

Charlotte burst out laughing. "Together? As in Dev and I in bed? Good God, no. Not ever. That would be like fucking a brother...ugh, I'll need plenty of brandy to wash away that thought."

"But...but you, ah, lived with each other for years," said Eliza, disbelief warring with desperate joy. Grayson and Charlotte weren't lovers and never had been?

"We did. No offense, Lady Eliza, but he just isn't my preference. I like very tall, very broad men with a rougher edge. Dev is too aristocratic. Too bookish. Unfortunately, finding a large, strapping submissive man is about as easy as finding an honest politician. So I spend my evenings wielding crops and whips downstairs instead. Which is where I should be right now."

An idea sprang into her head, one so outrageous, she almost tumbled over. "Do you...do you think I could watch?"

Charlotte tilted her head and gave her a thoughtful look. "To enjoy, or something else? I hear you administer a perfect slap."

Her cheeks burned. "I know Grayson has certain, ah,

needs. I want to see how it is done. Then I'll know if maybe I could do it for him, or not ever."

"You're serious, then? Lady or no, I will never consent to assisting you if your damned sensibilities are going to take over again and you hurt him by pulling right back. Because this time would be so much worse, when Dev has seen what happiness could be like."

Eliza let out a slow breath. It was time to lay all her cards out on the table, and that meant her past regrets as well. Everyone, including herself, deserved the truth even if it was uncomfortable. "I was such a fool. Pulling back hurt me as well as him. I'm not delicate and ladylike, I'm bold and bossy. I love instructing him. I love being in control, and I'm so blasted tired of hiding it."

Charlotte grinned. "Very well. Come with me."

After fetching her mask, Eliza followed Charlotte downstairs and through a discreet back door into the club proper. Soon they were walking around a familiar corner, and her steps faltered slightly as she looked at the same room Grayson had been in with all the couples. Fortunately, Charlotte kept walking and pushed open the door to the room next to it. This one was a little smaller and had a wide padded bench, a tray of whips, crops and toys, and a curtained off square in the far right corner. "Can I sit in there?"

"Make yourself comfortable," said Charlotte with a wave. "My first gentleman friend will be here very shortly."

Eliza barely had time to sit down and pull the curtain mostly closed, when a naked man appeared in the doorway, his head bowed. He wore a numbered mask, his brown hair touched with silver, as were the curls dusting his chest. An older gentleman but with the strong thighs and thick wrists of an expert rider, a short but very thick cock dangling between his legs.

"Charlotte, ma'am, may I enter your domain?"

"You may," said Charlotte crisply, and Eliza could only watch in amazement as the woman discarded her robe to reveal a very seductive Amazonian warrior costume: black leather corset, shoulder plates, gold forearm cuffs, and flat sandals with straps that wound around her legs from ankle to knee. She looked magnificent, so confident and powerful. "Are you well, pet?"

"I am indeed. And honored that you agreed to see me."

"Good," purred Charlotte, briefly cupping the man's cheek as he stood in the center of the room. "Before we begin, I must tell you I have a colleague who wants to watch and learn. Do you consent or wish her to leave? In this instance, neither decision is wrong."

He smiled shyly. "If it pleases you, I consent for the lady to stay."

"All right. Come out, milady. A better view here."

Eyes wide, and very grateful for the mask she wore, Eliza slipped out from behind the curtain. "Thank you both."

Charlotte nodded and turned to the man. "Why are you here?"

"To see you."

"No," said Charlotte, picking up a riding crop and slapping it against her thigh. "Tell me why you are really here, pet. Only then can I give you what you crave."

The gentleman quivered, then clasped his hands. "I'm so tired. Every day I give orders. Every day I must be…another. My wife, my children, my brothers and sisters, my mother… every day, they all want, so I must be that man. And I'm so damned tired."

"You wish me to be in charge. To make decisions that will bring you great pleasure."

"Please," he said hoarsely. "Please."

"Then get onto the bench, hands and knees, eyes down."

Fascinated, Eliza watched as Charlotte strolled around

the room like a queen while the gentleman settled himself on the bench. She was so sure of herself, her smile bright and her shoulders back, utterly unashamed of who she was…and in turn this man had been able to relax and share who he was, too.

"Can I…" said Eliza hesitantly. "Can I ask a question?"

"Certainly," said Charlotte.

"Sir," she said, the words tumbling out in a rush. "Do you like pain? I mean, does it bring you greater pleasure if you are whipped for example?"

The man turned his head, his smile gentle. "I like it very much, ma'am. It brings me astonishing clarity of mind, and I can let go of what troubles me. Then I can come. My only regret is not requesting time with Miss Charlotte earlier. Finding a lady who understands and is unafraid, no, not just unafraid but *delights* in her desires…is a miracle. I am most grateful."

Eliza collapsed into a chair, her mind awhirl. But through that burst excitement. If she watched Charlotte carefully, she could learn how to proceed. How to revel in her own needs and desires, and in turn free Grayson to revel in his. To transform their marriage once and for all into a partnership where all sexual needs were met, and in a way that was safe and loving.

"Then please, Charlotte…sir…do begin."

Charlotte circled the bench, one hand caressing the gentleman's back and bottom. "Such beautiful skin. I do enjoy marking it. This evening you will count to ten for me, but you may not move or come without my permission."

"Yes, ma'am."

The first few blows of the riding crop were light, barely leaving an imprint on the man's hair-dusted thighs. But on the third, a slap hard enough to pinken the fleshy part of his bottom, he shivered. Charlotte paused, stepping away.

Oh my. A form of *punishment*. Charlotte didn't say a word, nor was she unkind, but the act was unmistakable. And yet the man wasn't angry or sad, only more visibly excited at this evidence that he did not control the situation.

When Charlotte continued she was harsher, blows four through seven turning her guest's bottom bright red. His panting breaths were audible, his voice as he counted increasingly scratchy and raw, but true to his oath, he did not move.

"Milady," said Charlotte, pausing to rotate her wrist. "You'll note how I do not hit the same spot twice. Nor do I aim for the tailbone or lower back. This is discipline, not abuse; I have no desire to cause injury."

"You are very skilled," Eliza replied softly, transfixed and more than a little aroused.

The eighth and ninth blows raised welts, and the gentleman sobbed as he counted. But his engorged cock bobbed against his stomach, the head glistening with pre-come, while the muscles in his forearms and thighs strained with the effort of remaining still.

Finally, Charlotte landed the last blow, a ferocious strike that broke the skin and brought a thin trail of blood to the surface. The man's "ten" was a guttural cry of ecstasy, and when Charlotte raised him from the bench so he knelt, slid her hand around his cock and ordered him to come, he coated the bench with his seed, his head thrown back to reveal tearstained cheeks and a smile so joyful, so serene, it almost felt too personal and private to watch.

"That was perfect, my lovely," murmured Charlotte, as she cuddled the man against her and stroked his hair. "Now, how do you show gratitude?"

Moaning, the gentleman pressed his face between Charlotte's legs, eagerly lapping her pussy and professing his thanks over and over.

Stumbling to her feet, her own pussy so wet and throbbing she could scarcely bear it, Eliza raised her hand in farewell. The other woman smiled knowingly and waved her away.

Back in the hallway, Eliza slumped against the cool wall, her heart pounding. The thought had been there for a while, and only strengthened this morning in the office with Grayson. But after that erotic demonstration, she knew without a doubt that false, timid, proper Eliza could never exist again.

For Grayson's fulfillment, she would gift him the pain-infused pleasure he needed.

And in turn, she would finally be free.

Chapter Six

Construction for the Midsummer Night festivities was progressing beautifully. But even the secondary ballroom—usually the home of the pirate ship—being transformed into an enchanted forest couldn't improve his mood.

Devil inhaled heavily, trying not to notice how the red, orange, and gold silk-draped wood pretending to be a bonfire resembled Eliza's hair. How the silver urns reminded him of the flecks in her eyes. And he failed utterly.

His wife had listened all too well when he'd stupidly turned away from her comfort and told her to leave. He'd barely seen her for days, not even in his office, and any moment he expected her to announce the next carriage outing would be her returning to Lincolnshire permanently.

"Dev. Dev!" bellowed Vice from behind him. "You have a visitor, thank God, so you can get the fuck out from under my feet."

"In my office?"

"No. The harem says that room needs a thorough scrubbing, so Sin has made his private parlor available."

Devil frowned but turned and left the ballroom. He wasn't expecting any visitors, and no suppliers had made appointments to see him. Curiosity overwhelmed, he almost ran to Sin's parlor, just remembering to slow down and walk through the door like someone who still possessed all their faculties.

"Hello, Gray."

Shock froze him to the spot, and he could only stare as his once-beloved older brother Peter, Viscount Upton, hesitantly approached him. Eventually he found his tongue. "What… what are you doing here?"

"Your wife arrived on my doorstep and insisted I accompany her back here," said Peter, his voice oddly hoarse, and his face strained. "I thought she might shoot me if I did not. Fiery little baggage, isn't she?"

A boulder lodged in his throat. *Eliza had done this?* "Yes. Yes she is. I'm not sure—"

"I invited Lord Upton," said a brisk voice to his right, "because it is long past time you spoke."

Devil turned, drinking in the welcome sight of Eliza. She was here. She hadn't left him. And she had brought him a gift beyond price.

Taking a moment to compose himself, he looked again at Peter. His brother remained taller and broader, but the Deveraux black hair was there in abundance, and Deveraux green eyes stared back at him with equal hesitancy and intense study. "I see."

"I'm very glad she did, Gray," said Peter. "So perhaps we could talk for a bit and I could beg your forgiveness."

"For what?" he replied slowly, resisting the urge to pinch himself at this miracle taking place. "You weren't even here when Reyburn disowned me. You were traveling the continent."

"That's no excuse," snapped his brother, pressing his fist to his mouth for a long moment before continuing. "What he did…Christ. When I found out, I hated him so much. But you'd gone, and I didn't know where. Nobody knew. And then you surfaced again, with this place. I wanted to come and see you, but I was too ashamed. As for your wedding, I will never forgive myself for refusing your invitation. I wanted to come. But bloody Reyburn said he would have me press-ganged into the Navy if I did…and I was too damned cowardly to stand against him."

"Upton—"

"Peter. I'm just Peter to you."

Devil closed his eyes. "I missed you. So much. But I wasn't fit for the likes of you. You've always been the better man. Angel to my Devil."

"Horseshit. You're my brother. You always have been, and you always will be."

He blinked, his eyes burning. "Reyburn won't like it."

"Reyburn can shove a hot poker up his arse. He can shove his title up there, too. Not that it is worth much anymore, the damned bastard is near bankrupt. I don't even know what I'm going to do with the estates. Sell the unentailed ones, I guess, but I'm lumped with the rest. A most attractive package for a prospective bride, a penniless title and failing properties."

"So you're not married?" said Eliza. "I forgot to ask before."

Peter sighed. "No. I'll have to find an heiress. They'll be lining up for miles now, especially with me as part of the deal."

"Can't see why you would be a problem, Peter," said Devil, frowning.

His brother suddenly grinned, a wicked, mischievous memory straight from their childhood. "As it turns out, little brother, you are not the only Deveraux with, ah, tastes other than the norm. I adore the ladies, but sometimes I, um, rather enjoy the company of a man as well. I'm planning to tell Reyburn and his cronies at the next ball he hosts."

Amusement welled, and soon Devil couldn't hold it in. Rocking on his feet, his whole body shaking and tears running down his cheeks, he laughed until his stomach hurt. Peter clapped him on the back, he returned the gesture, and it turned into a hug—for one long, glorious moment time wound back and they were Pete and Gray again, two brothers against the world as they held each other tightly and mourned their lost years.

Finally, he stepped back. "You must join Fallen. You'll meet all sorts of likeminded men and women, and as a bonus, the news might finish Reyburn off."

Eliza snorted, her own eyes suspiciously bright. "What Grayson means is that you are always welcome here, Lord Upton. Would you care for tea?"

Peter's shoulders slumped. "On another occasion, I would like nothing more. But alas today, I have a meeting with my bankers that I cannot miss. I have asked for the truth about my finances, and I am very much afraid they are going to give it to me. But, best to know the ground before you build the castle, correct?"

"If you need funds," said Devil, "I'd be happy to—"

"Very kind, but no thank you. Just have the brandy ready next time. A special bottle, about three feet tall."

"Right you are," he replied, holding out his hand. Peter shook it firmly, clapped him again on the shoulder, then strode from the parlor.

Incredulous, he blinked at Eliza. "Did that just happen?"

She smiled hesitantly. "It did. I hope you aren't angry at me for interfering, but Charlotte said your brother was a decent man, and he really does seem to be one."

"Wait a minute. Excuse me? You were talking to Charlie?"

Eliza's gaze locked on his, her cheeks turning pink. "Another decent person who loves you. You aren't alone, Grayson, even if it sometimes feels like you are. And damn it, you can't keep shoving people away so you won't be hurt again. That shoves away the potential happiness, as well."

Rubbing his jaw to buy a moment, Devil swallowed hard. "It was so good to see Peter. Thank you for doing that for me. I wish there was something I could do for you. Not your family, but you."

"There is."

"Name it, and it is yours. There is still time to go to Mayfair if you want to shop. Gowns, jewels, slippers, bonnets, whatever you want."

"Bah. Not interested. What I want is something infinitely more rewarding."

Devil considered. "A trip? Vienna is lovely this time of year. Or Rome."

She took a deep breath, her shoulders straightening, like she was preparing for battle. "Actually, what I want is you. Upstairs, naked, and bent over. You require discipline, Grayson, and I have a brand new cane I am eager to try out."

All the air whooshed from his lungs. "I beg your pardon?"

His ears had to be deceiving him. His wife had not just oh-so-casually said she wished to use a cane on him, had she?

"You heard me," she said in a steely voice. Then she circled him, one hand caressing his backside, and he groaned, shuddering in anticipation as his cock hardened to stone. "Upstairs. Now."

• • •

The leather of the corset was surprisingly soft and sensual against her skin, and the built-in stays cupped and pushed her breasts high, her nipples barely covered by the bodice. Her legs were bare, and she wore heeled slippers on her feet.

All in all, she felt very seductive. Powerful. Free.

Strolling out of the antechamber and into the main room, new slender cane in hand, Eliza paused to enjoy the sight of her naked husband on the four-poster bed. At the present time he lay flat on his stomach, his chin resting on his forearms, but as soon as she cleared her throat, he went straight up onto his hands and knees.

"Eliza," he breathed, his green eyes glowing. "You look magnificent."

The compliment warmed her to her toes, but this insubordination simply wouldn't do.

Twirling the cane with a flick of her wrist, she slapped it hard on the bed a mere inch from his hand. "You may refer to me as…Lizzie. Now, get off the bed. I want you standing next to it, your hands braced on the left side post."

A less keen observer might have missed the quiver of excitement he couldn't quite suppress as he quickly obeyed her instruction. But he couldn't hide the reaction of his cock; it was already hugely swollen and bobbing against his flat belly. "Yes, Lizzie."

"And what is your word if you wish me to stop?"

Grayson stared at her in astonishment. Then as understanding dawned, with such love and overwhelming tenderness, she swallowed a lump in her throat. "Fire. Like the most wonderful woman in the world."

"Very well. But before we begin, there is one more thing I must do."

Smiling to herself, she reached into her bodice and pulled out the fifteen thousand pound bank draft he had written.

And she tore it to pieces.

"Lizzie! But…"

"This is not about money, Grayson. It is about pleasure. Happiness. Me being me, and you being you, and both of us being proud of it. Do you understand?"

He swallowed hard. "Yes, ma'am. I'm…I'm getting there."

Nodding in approval, Eliza reached out and trailed the end of the cane along his skin. Slowly, gently, up and down, around in a circle, teasing his hair-roughened thighs and forearms, his smooth, muscled back. Without warning she struck, one quick, sharp blow across the back of his thigh.

He gasped. "*Yes*."

Again and again she stroked him with the cane then hit, varying the spot—his shoulder, forearm, thighs with pale pink marks, never settling into a rhythm or pace, keeping him on the edge but not touching him where he wanted it most. "Are you all right, Grayson?"

Her husband moaned. "Please don't stop."

"Does your cock hurt? It looks very, very hard. So full of come. What would you give to have me take that in my mouth? To thrust it deep into my wet pussy?"

"Anything."

Flicking her wrist as Charlotte had taught her in their sessions, Eliza brought the cane down hard on his backside, leaving a red imprint. "Please don't stop, *Lizzie*. Anything, *Lizzie*."

Grayson jerked, his breathing deliciously ragged. "Forgive me, Lizzie. I wasn't thinking. Only feeling. It's so damned good. I've never been harder in my life…ah Christ."

"You like it there, don't you? Right on that fleshy curve of your backside. Two lovely red patches," she mused, admiring her handiwork and crouching down to kiss each mark. He writhed under her touch, but when she gently parted his flesh and licked the puckered opening of his back entrance, he nearly crushed the bedpost with his grip. Well. Charlotte certainly did know everything.

"Fuck," he swore, roughly. "I'm going to come, Lizzie. If you do that again, I'll come all over the quilt."

"I think not," she said sternly, glad he couldn't see her teary smile. "You are not allowed to come. Not until I say so. Understand?"

"Yes, Lizzie. I…fuck. Christ."

Eliza *tsked*. "Such language in front of your innocent, prim and proper wife. All I did was stroke your balls and cock with my hand. But you were telling me the truth. Your cockhead is already slick with moisture. And yet I'm not done."

Swish. Crack. Swish. Crack.

The two swift, harsh blows almost landed on top of each other, raising faint welts on the firm flesh of his backside. Grayson cried out her name in a sobbing, guttural voice, his whole body shaking as he visibly fought to remain upright and not slump against the post or onto the bed, to give his cock that last little bit of direct stimulation it needed to push him over the edge into orgasm.

If she were honest, the feeling was mutual. Her nipples were so rigid and swollen the soft leather felt like sack cloth, and her pussy was so wet juices were gathering in the red curls guarding her mound and trickling down her inner thighs.

"Please, Lizzie," he whispered. "Please, darling, please let me come."

Nudging his shoulder, she made him turn around and look at her. His face was damp with sweat, his cheeks flushed, his eyes pure emerald fire, burning with need and violent arousal and adoration. "No. You must earn your orgasm, my love, and attend to my breasts and pussy."

Eliza lay down on the bed, cupping her breasts in her hands, and spreading her thighs. Eagerly, he knelt between them, tugging down the top of her corset until her taut nipples popped out, taking them into his hot mouth and sucking hard. She whimpered, squirming on the soft quilt, knowing in absolute delight that he wouldn't stop unless she instructed it.

When her nipples were stimulated to that perfect point just below pain, she touched his forehead. Grayson moaned, scrambling farther down the bed so he could have direct access to her soaking wet pussy. Burying his face between her legs, he licked her slit, lapped at her clit, then shoved his tongue deep inside her. At one point he even mimicked her action and rubbed his tongue over her back entrance, making her shout his name as jolts of ecstasy raced from one acute pleasure point to the next.

But she couldn't wait any longer. Again, she touched his forehead, and he halted.

"Lizzie?"

"I want you. Now," she said throatily. "Hard and deep."

Grayson nodded, his smile an endearing mixture of lust and love and pure relief. Carefully, he fitted his cock to her pussy entrance, paused for the tiniest moment, then thrust home.

"Yes. More. Give me more," she cried, wrapping her legs around his waist, one hand on his shoulder and one threaded through his hair, gripping and scratching and tugging him as he plunged and withdrew over and over, gasping her name like a prayer.

All too soon her inner muscles tightened, clamping down on his cock as she reached the edge and hurtled over it, screaming and screaming as the most violent, prolonged climax of her life surged through her body. Seconds later he joined her, bucking and writhing as he came, long, hard gushes of seed filling her to overflowing.

He collapsed on top of her and she welcomed his weight and bulk, stroking his neck and crooning nonsense words of appreciation and praise in his ear.

Eventually he lifted his head, blinking at her like he'd finally woken from the longest sleep. "Eliza. That was...my God. How did you know?"

If she'd had the energy, she might have laughed. "Education is key. I took lessons."

"Lessons in using a cane?"

"Amongst other things."

Grayson reached up and stroked the backs of his fingers against her cheek. "You must care for me a great deal to do this. To change."

"I love you more than anything in the world, and always will. But I'm not changing. I'm discovering. As I said before, when I am my true self, you can be your true self, and we are both happy. We are both *free*. Well, I'm nearly free…" Eliza finished awkwardly.

"Are you thinking of your mother?"

"Yes. I couldn't bear it if anything happened to Papa, or the academy and its teachers and students. But if you write Mother another blasted bank draft, she wins easily."

He grinned, his eyes suddenly alight with wickedness. "Eliza Jean Brimley Deveraux. Surely you know that nothing with me and money is ever *easy*. Naturally a sum of fifteen thousand pounds comes with certain non-negotiable conditions."

Laughter bubbled. "Such as?"

"Whatever you see fit to impose. I bow to you in all things…as will your dear mother."

Eliza stared at him, joy unfurling in her heart at the resolute support to take control of her own life. "I'd like for you to accompany me to the academy, then."

"That, my darling, beloved Lizzie, is a show I wouldn't miss for the world."

. . .

The Brimley Finishing Academy was a stately property, one large central building, two smaller wings on either side, and a lovely landscaped garden in the front. But as their carriage moved down the gravel driveway, Eliza truly regretted her lack of brandy on the journey with Grayson and Lord Upton. After all the talking, this was the day of action. And she didn't know if she had the courage to face down her mother once and for all.

Grayson cleared his throat. "You know, Eliza, that signage is most impressive. Delightful, Decorous, *and* Demure in preparation for excellent marriages? The academy is not getting just reward for its contribution to the fabric of English society."

She sniffed, her lips twitching at his effort to distract her. "Oh, hush up. That foolish philosophy will be the first to go."

"So what will it be, then? Saucy, Sinful, and Seductive? You'll have gentlemen beating down the door for such a wife…" he replied, his words trailing off in a look of tender bliss as she discreetly pinched him.

Gracious, that was the least of what she'd done to Grayson throughout the night. She'd had him again and again, most recently when the sun rose and spilled orange light into their bedchamber. Her new favorite toy, the cane, was well broken in. As were the lengths of satin she'd used to restrain his wrists, and the delightful solid gold miniature balls she'd tried for herself. She ached all over; Grayson's skin was a tapestry of faint marks and scratches. But the haunted look had left his eyes, the tension released from his shoulders. He had found peace, and in turn, so had she.

"Oh, for God's sake, you two," said Lord Upton, hurling a cushion at them from the opposite side of the carriage as it came to a halt. "I will cast up my accounts if you don't immediately cease and desist. And will you please explain why I'm at the bloody Brimley Finishing Academy of all places…damnation, Gray. You are smiling that smile. I don't know how our governess ever fell for it; it only ever meant Deveraux trouble."

Grayson snorted as he assisted her from the carriage. "Peter, I'm shocked. How could you possibly think three Deverauxs descending on the Brimley Finishing Academy would result in such a thing?"

"Because trouble is what we always did best. And I strongly suspect Lady Eliza is very much a Deveraux in that respect."

"I'm sure I don't know what you mean, dear brother-in-law," said Eliza, widening her eyes innocently. "I do have a plan, though. And I promise it will be worth the early start to travel here."

"Lord Grayson! Eliza! What an, er, unexpected delight," called Lady Brimley as she flung open the door and appeared on the academy's front steps.

Perspiration misted on the back of her neck, but Eliza took a deep breath and forced herself to be calm. "Hello, Mother," she said as coolly as she could. "We've come to deliver a draft for fifteen thousand pounds."

Lady Brimley blinked, a small victory in itself. "Oh, how wonderful! Do come in…and greetings to you also, Lord Upton! Well I never. What a treat to have a supremely eligible viscount visit us as well."

Lord Upton winced, clearly unhappy at the reminder, but after exchanging a glance, the three of them followed the countess inside and into the charming, if slightly shabby, parlor. The academy sorely needed redecorating. At the top of the list: new paint, thick rugs, and curtains not coated in years of damp and dust.

"I'm so glad you finally did your duty, Eliza. You are useful after all," continued Lady Brimley, holding out her hand. "Now, where is that draft? I'd hate to hold you up from your busy lives."

Eliza laughed at the familiar tactic, an order masquerading as concern. "Are you trying to get rid of us, Mother?"

Lady Brimley faltered. "Excuse me?"

"We've come for a nice, long visit. To look around and discuss the terms of the draft."

"Terms? What…what on earth are you talking about?"

"Business," said Eliza, tilting her head. "You know, I really have learned so much working side by side with my husband on the ledgers and such. Wouldn't you say, Grayson?"

"Without question, my dear," said her husband, his lips twitching. "You really are a master tradeswoman now. I've never seen terms so expertly crafted."

Lady Brimley scowled. "This is just plain disrespectful."

"I would have thought taking money from a school far worse," mused Eliza. "But in any case, you will only receive the draft if you agree to the conditions and sign a contract that I prepared. The day of reckoning is here, Mother."

"Eliza! How dare you speak to me in such a tone. The insolence. And in front of Lord Grayson."

"I didn't hear any insolence," said Grayson. "Did you, Upton?"

The viscount shook his head, his face a study of polite blankness. "Not a word."

"Well," Lady Brimley spluttered. "Well—"

"As I was saying," said Eliza, the knowledge she had the unwavering support of her husband and brother-in-law, if needed, boosting her confidence higher. "There are certain conditions you must meet to save the academy. Firstly, the books shall be audited by Grayson on a quarterly basis."

Her mother nodded reluctantly. "Of course."

"Secondly, a board of governors will be appointed. Lord Upton will chair this board for the next five years and will be paid an annual sum of twenty thousand pounds to do so."

The viscount inhaled sharply, shock and something that looked very much like hope in his eyes, warring with pride. "My lady?"

Eliza smiled. "It's just as we discussed, my lord. Apart from the payment. I thought your suggested amount was most inadequate, and my husband concurred. Tell him, Grayson."

"You'll be an excellent chair, Upton. Honorable and trustworthy. Such a position and service must be compensated appropriately," said Grayson, nodding solemnly.

"Indeed it must," said Lady Brimley, her eyes gleaming. "And perhaps I—"

"No," said Eliza, the word dropping like a cannonball into

the room. "You will have no access to academy funds. By the by, your stipend will be two hundred pounds annually."

"That is outrage—"

"You will be patron in name only, Mother. For public events and so forth."

"*What?*" Lady Brimley screeched, her cheeks taking on a most unbecoming plum hue.

Eliza coughed to disguise a laugh. Thank heavens none of the Delightful, Decorous, and Demure could see her now; this was becoming almost enjoyable.

"I am not finished," she continued. "Thirdly, the curriculum of this finishing school, and indeed the purpose and heart of it, will be decided by the board. Let me make it plain that the Delightful, Decorous, and Demure nonsense will not continue. The young ladies who graduate from here will be accomplished, strong of character, instilled with a sense of belief in themselves and their abilities, and not under any circumstances will they be encouraged to marry a man they do not have a connection of the heart with. It is 1814. It is time for a more modern outlook."

Lady Brimley swooned, delicately sliding from her chair and ending up in a perfectly arranged heap on the ground.

"I think," said Grayson, raising one eyebrow, "that she took that rather well."

Eliza sank back onto her own chair, incredulous she'd finally said the words. Her head was spinning, but it felt as though the heaviest of loads had been lifted from her shoulders. "Give her two to three minutes; her fainting spells never last longer than that. It's in the rule book."

"Duly noted. By the by, my dear, what a speech. If I had a hat, I would take it off to you."

"Are the two of you in earnest?" said Lord Upton with a small frown. "I want no charity. That is an excessively large sum of money to chair a governance board."

"Except you have to deal with my mother," said Eliza wryly. "In which case you will earn every penny. And you never know, perhaps in the course of your time here, you might meet a young lady who suits admirably well. I cannot guarantee, er, Saucy, Sinful, and Seductive though."

"More's the pity."

Grayson burst out laughing. "You'll be hunted like a fox, brother. On second thought, twenty thousand might not be enough."

A soft groan sounded from the floor, and they quieted as Lady Brimley made a performance of sitting up and rubbing her elbow. "You're all still here. And not one of you rushed to my assistance."

"We were quite certain you would survive, Mother," said Eliza, rolling her eyes. "And you haven't signed the contract yet."

"I will not sign the beastly thing."

"Your decision, of course. But it would be such a shame if a story about the missing money appeared in the scandal sheets. Why, everyone in the *ton* would know in a heartbeat."

Grayson nodded. "Amazing how much detail is included. Damned anonymous sources."

"You…you…unconscionable…" Lady Brimley snarled, then her shoulders slumped. "Give me the contract."

As soon as they had the signed and sealed document, she, Grayson, and Lord Upton strolled back outside into the summer sunshine.

"Hell," said her brother-in-law. "Things are certainly looking up."

Eliza grinned and tucked her arm through Grayson's. He looked back at her with such pride her heart felt like it might burst. Everything had been wrong. And now it was so right.

"That they are," she replied. "That they blasted well are."

Epilogue

The ballroom looked spectacular as an enchanted forest for their pagan festivities, but nothing came close to Eliza.

His own Lizzie.

She wore green silk, the shade like new spring leaves, fashioned into a Grecian tunic that draped over one shoulder and left the other bare. Her unruly hair tumbled in waves down her back, and perched on her head was a circlet of cream roses. Diamonds adorned her throat and wrists, alongside a new ruby betrothal ring that he'd purchased to celebrate their new start. Like Vice, and Sin and Grace, she no longer wore a mask, so she was clearly identified as a co-owner of Fallen.

"Did I remember to tell you, you look magnificent?" Devil whispered into her ear.

"Only about sixty-five times," she murmured back, her eyes shining.

"Not nearly enough. You'll be the best fairy queen ever seen in the history of England."

"I must say, you make a very fine consort. Although if those ladies don't stop salivating over your bare chest and the way those breeches cup your backside, I'm going to get cross."

"Didn't even see them," he said honestly. "Do you want me to fetch a shirt?"

Eliza splayed a hand over his chest. "No. I want them to see and envy what belongs to me. Ah look. There is Vice, and my throne."

Smiling, he followed her over to a wide raised dais with two velvet-covered gold thrones sitting atop it. Vice sat sprawled in one, dressed in cream breeches, a bejeweled cloak, and a ruby-and-silver crown atop his head—although how long that would stay with Prinny hovering at his feet and making pointed comments about usurpers was anyone's guess. Grace and Sin stood to one side, arms wrapped around each other, both dressed in brown and green silk as wood sprites. Though Grace's delicate blond beauty looked far more believable than her small mountain of a husband.

"Lady Eliza!" said Vice, waving them over. "Your throne awaits, my dear. And don't you look splendid. Too bad about Dev, I do think he would have been better as a rock."

Withdrawing her cane from a jeweled scabbard at her waist, Eliza pointed it in Vice's direction. "Choose your words carefully, knave. They may be your last."

Vice held up both hands. "I might be persuaded to surrender. And yet, the way you swing that cane leads me to believe I know the exact reason for your husband's recent good humor, and that perhaps I should fight on."

Devil mock-scowled. "Find your own wife."

Just for a moment his friend grimaced, a kind of aching world weariness he never would have imagined Vice even thinking, let alone expressing. Startled, he stepped forward, but in the blink of an eye, Vice leaped from the dais down into the crush of people, talking and laughing, and passionately kissing several masked and half-naked women.

"I worry about him," said Eliza quietly, as he helped her

up onto her throne. "He's not nearly as carefree and hedonistic as he makes out, is he?"

"Hedonistic, yes," he replied. "Vice puts both Sin and I to shame when it comes to indulging in raw pleasure. But carefree? No. I think you are right."

"Hmmm. Well, now that Vice has vacated his throne, do you want to come and sit in it?"

Devil shook his head. "Not my place, Lizzie. Too far away from you and your cane. I'd rather sit at your feet where you can stroke my hair and whisper wicked things in my ear."

"If you do that, everyone will see. And they'll know."

"Yes," he said, taking a deep breath and letting it out slowly. "I want them to know. I'm not ashamed anymore. I'm happy. Like you said in our chamber, I have also found myself, and I'm free. Society be damned. When has pleasing them and following the rules ever helped anything anyway?"

Eliza laughed. "Touché, my love. Well then, get yourself up here, there is a prime spot awaiting you."

Climbing up, he settled at her feet, leaned his head against her thigh and sighed with contentment. His gaze traveled the length and breadth of the forest ballroom, but shockingly, he didn't see disdain or disgust on anyone's faces. In fact, masked men and women were nodding and smiling, some raising their champagne glasses in a toast.

"They're accepting it," he said wonderingly.

"Well of course they are," she said, smoothing his hair in her supremely calming way. "Because you and Sin and Vice accepted them. You've never judged or mocked their desires, so they are returning the favor. Fallen really is a sanctuary for everyone, including you, and you helped make it what it is."

Devil smiled and raised his hand in a little wave to the crowd, and they cheered. Peter, their newest member, raised his hands above his head and applauded, a huge smile on his face. Interestingly, a very wealthy-looking couple stood next to him with rather proprietary hands on his waist. It seemed his brother had already made some new friends.

That was all you needed really. The love of the right person, good friends, a place of your own, and acceptance of your true self.

Well, that and a very sturdy cane.

About the Author

Nicola Davidson worked for many years in communications and marketing as well as television and print journalism, but hasn't looked back since she decided writing wicked historical romance was infinitely more fun. When not chained to a computer she can be found ambling along one of New Zealand's beautiful beaches, cheering on the champion All Blacks rugby team, history geeking on the internet, or daydreaming. If this includes chocolate—even better!

Keep up with Nicola's news on Twitter, Facebook, or her website www.nicola-davidson.com

If you love erotica, one-click these hot Scorched releases…

HOOKED
a *Viking Bastards* novel by Christina Phillips

I like my sex dirty and disposable. I'm not into commitment or chicks who want more than one night. Until *she* walks into my life. Classy, rich and so out of my league it's crazy. A week together should get her out of my system, but this good girl is so bad when we're all alone and I can't get enough of her. But there's no way a princess can live in my world and I sure as hell won't live in hers...

RUTHLESS
a *Playboys in Love* novel by Gina L. Maxwell

People call me Ruthless for a reason. Whether I'm in the court room or in the bedroom, my reputation is well-earned. I'm either working hard, working out, or working my way into some woman's panties. But none of them share my particular kink, and I walk away feeling unsatisfied. Until I met *her*.

THE LIST
a *List* novel by Tawna Fenske

Brainy soil scientist Cassie Michaels has spent her whole life longing to be more adventurous. To make herself more interesting, Cassie invented stories about her wild sex life—stories she's expected to retell in vivid detail at a bachelorette party. Her attempt to catalog her biggest whoppers goes horribly wrong when she spills wine on her laptop and lands in Simon Traxel's computer shop with her sexy list frozen on the screen. Lucky for Cassie, Simon offers to help her out…with the computer AND by making Cassie's list of make-believe sexploits a reality!

LOVING HER ALPHAS
a novel by Ari Thatcher

After a wolf attacks Rayne Adler near her grandfather's lodge, the Whitmore brothers nurse her back to health. Unaware they are wolf-shifters, she finds each appealing in a different way. But, she's not at Shady Pines Lodge for romance, nor would she ever choose between them. The successful businesswoman is there only to refurbish the grounds and bring tourism back to the area. Caleb, Nick, and Dalton are thrilled to finally have found their mate in spunky Rayne Adler and will use everything in their power to persuade her that she was made for them. All three of them.

Made in the USA
Charleston, SC
29 January 2017